A B C D E F G H I J K L M N O P Q R S T U V W X Y Z . . .

Alphabetique

26 Characteristic Fictions

MOLLY PEACOCK

with illustrations by Kara Kosaka

 McClelland & Stewart

Library and Archives Canada Cataloguing in Publication
is available upon request.

Typeset in Tribute by M&S, Toronto
Printed and bound in China

McClelland & Stewart,
a division of Random House of Canada Limited,
a Penguin Random House Company
www.randomhouse.ca

1 2 3 4 5   18 17 16 15 14

For all who imagine alternate lives

for Joan Stein, late-life painter

&

for Mike

The Birth of a Genuine Article

 Nobody much noticed her as a child. Nobody's supposed to notice a small *a*. Born an athlete, she grew up on long, slender legs to her point, becoming a capital of quiet beauty. Now A was pregnant, ascending the Alps with her husband THE on their very last climb for a while—since even A-1 members of the Alpine Club never mountaineer in the third trimester.

THE threw her a rope. She caught it as auras of auroras sky-skipped around her, and THE sang out possible names for their little one, while the mountains echoed back:

"Alpenglow—glow-glow?"

"Apogee—gee-gee?"

"Something so . . . "—the altitude made it almost too hard for A to talk—" . . . so commonplace it's . . . extraordinary."

"An audacious appellation," her husband announced as she approached him. "That's what we need! How about Acrophile?"

For the apple of our amour? No! A didn't say.

As a little girl she couldn't wait to jump into things, to somersault behind an *e* to make an eagle fly, or pirouette before twin *p*s to make an apple pie. Oh, for the chance to leap three times and make an aardvark!

When she got a little older, she loved nothing better than to arrange an assortment of letters and cap them with herself, climbing up an *I*, then a *D*, then an *E* to send an idea into the world. But now she was shy to anticipate. She was expecting—but she tried to avoid expectation. *Naming a first child*, she despaired, *it's one of the most original acts of a lifetime.*

When they reached the crest at last, they perched and ate their snack of almonds and dried apricots. "How about Artichoke?" THE said blithely as he chewed. "Or Argyle?"

A tucked her point under the broad shoulders of his crossbar. "We need something almost invisible," she mused, "for our little anonymouse."

THE always napped at the summit, but A felt awakened to the child inside her. Aware of the one to come, she also remembered the child she'd been. It was a slow, slow avalanche of realizations.

She'd proceeded through her early years almost invisibly, except in the eyes of her Aunt AN. It was she who came to recognize wee a's abilities. "My acrobat," she would say to her niece, "my tiny mouse." AN, who was solitary, childless (and quite a bit older than A's astrologically mismatched, acrimonious parents) trained little a for her roles in life.

She taught her the arabesque, the front and back attitudes, the boost. AN's affection warmed A like a beloved angora sweater. The girl learned her bridge, her cannonball, her handstand, her headspring, her twirl.

But as the old woman became even older, her *A* began to lose its firm slant. Absorbed with tumbling lessons, her young apprentice hardly noticed. Eventually the valiant elderly article suffered such ague that the legs of her first letter collapsed. She was rushed to St. Anne's hospital, her surprised niece hovering at her side.

"Will I," A asked her ailing aunt, "collapse, too?"

"Highly unlikely. Remember, you're special, you have two jobs to do, unlike the rest of us. You're a letter, but you're an article as well. You make words, but like me you introduce them, too. You've got to learn to pace yourself. It's a long life."

A quaked at the prospect. Two roles—she'd never realized. She'd just pirouetted her way, protected by her elder.

"Put one foot in front of the other," ancient AN continued, nearly out of breath. "That's how to live."

As a child interprets adult wisdom, A decided then and there to be careful always, calculating each and every tumble. She would try her hardest never again to anticipate or leap.

Aunt AN went on for a while but began to lose her point. "You'll have to do it for me . . . " she whispered. "You can, you know . . . You're the genuine article."

After hearing those last words, young A descended in the battered hospital elevator to a life in the absence of the anchor of her world. Her parents were so absorbed in arguments she barely saw them. Her friends were uniting with vowels and locking themselves into the interiors of words. She found herself alone.

In anguish A joined the Alpine Club, to refresh herself in the mountain air. Everybody at the club went about their business, and nobody really noticed her—except THE.

"I've been watching you," he said. "You're the genuine article."

"Really?"

"Absolutely," he said.

Suddenly she leapt into his arms.

"That was unanticipated!"

"I know, I gave up anticipation," A answered. If you give up hope, you give up agony.

"Gave it *up*?" THE was incredulous. "But that's what articles *do*. We go before any person, place, or thing that needs an introduction."

"Well, I'm not only an article," A explained. "I'm also a letter. I prefer letter work, actually."

And so they began climbing together. A was in peak shape, THE certainly didn't have to be told.

One thing led to another . . .

❦

Now, while THE slept, A let her legs stretch, her point perk. Her aspirations, if she could admit she had them, glowed like ascending horizons. *Aunt AN, A thought, she had aplomb.* A felt a fizz of excitement and didn't quash it. She heard the merest suggestion of applause, and she smelled something, too. The perfume of her aunt's affection seemed to waft toward her.

Approval seemed to wrap around A, and just as she was relaxing, an outline appeared in the air. Gradually the outline filled in—it was the ghost of Aunt AN materializing, and her robust voice declared: A NAMER AS WELL AS A BEARER BE.

Just as A was about to call "Aunt AN!" the ghost smiled a beneficent smile, and waved, sailing off into the alpine mist.

When she heard him say, "Careful!" A realized THE had woken and, in the haze of her epiphany, he'd already helped her begin the downward slope.

"Whatever will we call our little appaloosa?" he worried again. A just concentrated on her footing.

At last, on the bench at the foot of the mountain, THE moaned, "I've never had to name anything before, let alone a child! I precede things. I'm a readiness . . ."

Slowly A said, "At the apex I—" could she bring it into being? "—apprehended . . . an apparition."

"Oh, what of?" THE asked, helping her off with her climbing gear, as if she encountered an apparition every day.

"The ghost of my Aunt AN appeared," she said, "and the sun was ablaze—this seems absurd, I know—and she said: A NAMER AS WELL AS A BEARER BE."

"Easy for an apparition to say," THE sighed.

"But we don't have to be specific!" A whispered. "We can name our little acorn something as elemental as our own names." The name could introduce each fresh thing as it rises into the air, could help each reach its apex . . .

And so she anticipated an advent necessary but not apparent, the sound that's uttered before an arrival—and taken by all as an article of faith.

"Let's call our little one AN," she said.

"Amen," THE happily breathed.

Portrait of a Letter as a Young B

Every morning the fonts gathered for breakfast in the big house before strolling to the studios in the woods where they did their work. But B was brand new and didn't understand that a font had to bustle in promptly to get the right seat at the right table. She came so late to breakfast on this breezy summer morning that there was no more room with any of the serif font groups—and no seats at any table of young fonts at all.

B was left to beg the last spot at a table of elderly sans serif Lucida Grandes.

"Hey, a Bembo in our midst," an old Grande said.

B smiled shyly.

"Welcome to the colony."

The long, large-flowered curtains ballooned. At the other tables, the breakfast chatter was all about font shows, font magazines, font editions, and font awards, and where a sans serif had the best chance. But with the Grandes, B calmly ate buttered bread, burnt bacon, and blackberries from a little bowl, recalling her grandmother's table.

Some of the fonts at the older Reject Table (as B came to think of it) resented every new font from Comic to Zapf, but others had a soft, dedicated glow. To entertain young Bembo, those oldsters talked about their work on *B*s. They still liked forming *better, best,* and the babbling triple *B* words like *bubble* and *bobble.* Soon the whole table unabashedly hummed, *"Baubles, bangles, bright shiny beads."*

After a few days the groups were so completely formed that B never got to sit with her peers. Even if she arrived early, she knew that barging into someone else's chair created a displacement, and forced the other font to sit with the blistering, bitter Times New Roman, as she once had to do. Times sat alone at the far-end table. In a single morning meal B learned how he loved his bite, like an acid sauna. His favorite words? *Bilious* and *blight.* B had barely thought about the honors for which Times so mordantly resented being ignored. How dare people call him "B-list." He was the best. He deserved the Bulitzer, the Brillium, and the Bovernor General's Award, not to mention the Bobel Prize.

After the ordeal of breakfast was over, B went to the press shop with relief. She spent the day becoming word after word, showing each its possibilities in a font from her graceful old family, Bembo. She had yet to choose her favorites, but *brillig* would be one of them.

Gradually B learned to love the old Grandes' stories of the beggars in the roads who voluntarily gave up everything— all blathering, all bothering, all bamboozling. B would have liked to avoid those vices, but she had not yet learned to go only toward the positive.

What she did learn that summer was to flee the negative, and she developed a Bembo prayer:

Don't let me B like U.
Don't let me B bitter.
Don't let me break against the wrong words
until I am bent and bruised.

B was so young, she had yet to learn to love. Right then she was just learning to work, and the old, benign rejected ones impressed her. Not much they had done was remembered anymore, but they were persevering at being, engaging themselves from *bramble* to *Beelzebub*.

Not to be bitter, Bembo prayed,
and just . . . just . . . to stay,
to do what I do.

So she bumbled through the rest of her summer.

C, the Softie

When there was something little c wanted to say, but he could only *see* it, he'd tell his father, Capital C, "I can feel the answer in my mind,"—and he could, a colt cavorting on a cold morning—"but I can't capture the words for it."

"Then you can't know the answer," Capital C would say. "You can't have an idea except in words." Yet c did too have ideas, whole constellations of them gamboling above him as he fell asleep . . .

Many years later, on the phone with his girlfriend, c's complicated thoughts concatenated. What could he say to her? Her voice was crisp as a cotton shirt, but c liked to curve his thoughts, to caress an idea's shoulders the way he liked to caress this girl. In his mind his longing curved, as much an opening as an enclosure, a harbor, like a *c* of land around water.

Then his father's credo crept into his mind: *Say it in words.*

"Ohhh," he whispered to her, "I love you." Those three words stood as confused as three capsized boys, lost, then captured, brought to shore, and charged with uncommitted crimes. His idea wasn't really *I-love-you*, but it was the closest he could come.

His girl took the words wrong. She couldn't help thinking of satin and crinolines, cream-colored bouquets, and a triple-tiered cake.

And so they were married.

And soon conceived their son.

But nothing ever crystallized between them, for confusion is necessary before conclusion, though c had yet to learn that, and Capital C had forgotten it, and c's wife, still crisp as lettuce, wilted at the very thought.

Not everything charms into words instantly. Some things whinny inside you or skitter out as hooves of color and later clang like horseshoes against a forge. Some things can't be crammed into a concept. They just have to be cried.

Excuses were concocted and clashes avoided. Their couples counselor could never persuade them into confrontation or cajole them into apologies. And so they crumpled . . .

But at his release from false commitment, c felt the value of his silences. He was a soft c, while Capital C had been hard, and his son's mother, now his ex-wife, was hard. Hard cs had their function in this world: they marched with hs to challenge and charge; they climbed with rs to crest and crown. They linked with ls to clatter. But soft c

preferred contemplation and slipping into a word to alter it, say from *sent* to *scent*.

Now, himself a grandfather in a cloud of spicy aftershave, c often did not bother to speak, except when he hooked his grandson under his arm and carried him up to bed. He tucked the boy in, but left the light on, and the child waited for c to go down to the kitchen. When grandpa returned with the kiddy cup of hot chocolate, he murmured to the curious child, *You see, little caterpillar, we soft cs don't like to close up our thoughts.* Then he adjusted the sipper spout and continued, *We like to leave things open and receive.*

D and His Deer

 D always felt, somehow or other, double. He was an upright line, but then again, he was a curve. When he looked in the mirror straight on, he saw the dapper features of the diplomat he was. But sideways, if he took off his horn-rimmed glasses, he imagined he could be taken for a rather distinguished Dame. He always saw both sides to everything.

Would he ever find his dæmon—the divine spirit within? Did he really have *one* spirit? D seemed to be singing a duet with himself.

Seeing both sides made him a champion procrastinator. D dilly-dallied. Waited till the last minute to decide anything. At every posting, he drove the staff crazy. But that was diplomacy.

Now dusk dropped on the gated embassy grounds. D flipped on his desk lamp, and the pool of light shut out the trees, looming and dissolving. D drew the drapes, deaf to the delicate drone of insect wings. He returned to his desk, trying to distract himself from a strange little pain that had come to him all his life, like a recurrent dream. (Except, he had to confess, he never dreamed.) The pain was a distinct tiny stab in a spot, well, what would you call that? D called it *down there*.

For years, since he was a little d, he considered all the options about this strange pain. It was nothing, really. He went long times between feeling it. Maybe it was too slight to worry about, but then again . . . At last D decided to see a doctor. As a matter of fact, he saw a number.

"Tell me your dreams," the first doctor said.

"Don't bother to ask me, I never dream," D said.

"In dreams begin responsibilities," the doctor quoted.

D demanded a referral.

"I've got a very specific pain," he said to the next doctor. He pointed to, well, down there.

"Your testicle," the physician said. Which required a test. Several. And more.

Finally the second doctor read all the results and announced, "Aha, a dermoid cyst." What? Inside the cyst were hair follicles and an eye-type thing with eyelashes and a tooth.

"Do you think I was a twin?" D wondered with a weird kind of delight as he examined the x-ray.

Well, the doctor wouldn't go that far. These dermoid cysts were usually removed in childhood. No reason, however, to remove it now. D wouldn't dream of having it removed! It explained everything! That slightly creepy

darling little creature in there *must* have been a twin, someone D had grown around as she dissolved. D was convinced it was a twin sister.

And D had absorbed her. Of course he wanted to keep her with him.

That very day, he had his first dream.

Exhausted after his discovery, he had returned to the embassy in the late afternoon. Unable to face his office, he diverted his steps from the front walk toward the deserted path on the grounds where no one ever seemed to stroll. He walked deeper into the woods. The path sloped into a shaded dimple in the earth.

It was dusk in the dell.

D heard the drone of insect wings. In the mottled light a dragonfly dove straight down. Up curved a damselfly.

Impulsively D lay down in the leaves in his three-piece suit and curled up like a praying divine, two hands under his chin. He felt himself melting a little. All the old bedevilments dispersed into a delicate dampness. The world softened from darkling to darling . . .

. . . A stately antlered stag appeared in the distance and slowly, with a calm command, walked closer until D could see that he wore a diamond necklace around his neck. The stag slowly bowed his head, doffed his entire rack of antlers, and raised his head up again, looking directly at D.

Now the deer was a doe! The doe blinked her eyes at D, as if waking. Then she donned the antlers, and turned and walked away . . .

D woke up ravenously hungry—and overjoyed.

He dusted himself off and drove straight to dinner. As he stared out the restaurant window, eating his dumplings, he wondered if responsibilities really do begin in dreams.

Maybe dreams are responsible to us, he thought.

He felt his sister inside him. She was the reason he was a debonair man, a man who understood that everything has two sides: inner/outer, yes/no. D thought both in lines as sharp as the creases in trousers, and in curves like the swirls of a skirt.

What do I really know? he asked himself. Only that he had woken strangely endeared to himself—and satisfied. Now he understood the necessity of delay. To wait, and then to discover. Never to have only one answer.

The napkin at the restaurant had come rolled inside a little sparkly ring. "Add this to my bill," he said to the waiter. And pocketed the little diadem as a reminder of the dyad he was.

E's Encyclopedia of Emotions

"What endeavor entices you?" E's family asked when she was very young. The queries from her uncle and her grandma and her first and second cousins, not to mention her parents, her siblings and great-grandpa, made her spin like a pinball in confusion. *Eeeek!*

But the rest of the e family all rolled calmly about their business in their enormous house, like stately marbles. They prided themselves on keeping small, keeping round, and keeping all together under one roof. Be the essence of one thing, they advised her. Pick an expertise and stick with it.

Perhaps you'd like to be an enthusiast? Choose one emotion and really develop it, they counseled. You could be eager, for instance. Eagerness is always attractive. Or, if you choose the negative, you could always follow in the path of Uncle e. His expertise is effrontery. Shameless nerve has its exponents.

But a restless enormity of emotions rainbowed over E. Choosing one of them for all existence? No! *I must be adopted,* she reasoned to herself. How could she be so unlike them and still be their kin? Yet her clan kept encouraging her toward a profession.

Three buds had begun to sprout along her spine, the beginnings of her adult arms. Perhaps they were meant to wrap around someone, E wondered. To high five with glee? Or wring elegiacally in sorrow?

To keep round and small, the family always nipped those buddings. But as E's came in, the more emotions she seemed to feel, and she wanted to keep on feeling them. However, around her family, she bunched herself up in a ball and rolled in as stately a way as she could, trying to mask her growing empathy.

She noticed how, more and more, she effervesced when she felt enraptured, and endured when she felt enraged. Occasionally, envy of her more compact siblings spasmed. Imagine choosing a lifetime of expertise in that!

To make sense of the elaborate possibilities, she decided to write them down, so she opened an Excel file. *Exaggerated*, she typed. *Emboldened. Embattled.*

One day E caught her reflection in one of the shining windows that the family never curtained—what had they to hide?—and discovered that she had elongated into elegance with enchanting arms that could express all the emotions she could ever encounter. She was entranced, and practiced waving to herself.

But of course she was alone with her reflection for barely a moment before she was surrounded again. "We've decided on a perfect choice for you," the uncle and grandma and great-grandpa and various siblings and cousins and her parents declared. "You could become an emoticon! Just roll down onto someone's keyboard and make a smiley face!"

"What!" She flailed her new arms in outrage. "I've never been more embarrassed!" she shouted. "Or more encumbered by your small ideas!"

The entire family was appalled. Had their little elf become an *enfant terrible*? Look how long her arms have grown, her grandma observed. She certainly couldn't be an emoticon now. Had she gone mad? the second cousins asked. Would she achieve excellence at all? her uncle worried.

"I want to edify and be edified—but emotionally," she explained excitedly. "I want to feel everything!"

Everything? The e family was stunned.

"Emotions are elements. I want to encounter every single one of them, like knowing the periodic table!" E whirled her arms like a windmill out of control, then stomped up to her bedroom, where she would have slammed the door had there been one. Why would anyone need privacy?

They all followed her, gathering around her bed, round-eyed and shocked to the core. There she was in the covers with her laptop, furiously working on her spreadsheet. *Enchanted*, she entered. *Elevated. Elastic. Energized.*

"You cannot be an e without being an expert," the uncle said.

"I won't espalier my life!" E declared.

E considered escaping. She had a brief wild fantasy of flying on the back of an eagle to a rainbow world of emotions where she could roll sybaritically in feelings for eternity— but her family bobbed around her. They were inescapable.

"Very well, I suppose you must experience every emotion, though the very thought depletes me," Grandma said. The whole family nodded vigorously. They could not embrace her ideas, but she was still estimable to them. How tall and rather efficient-looking she'd become.

I don't ever want to choose just one feeling, she thought, and typed *Erotic. Erroneous. Enmeshed.*

"Oh dear," Great-grandpa said. "You can't be enamored with everything."

"I want to feel ethical and feel embroiled and endorsed and . . ." She entered all these words in the spreadsheet. Then she made a new column and began entering definitions.

The next day she went out to experience the emotions she'd recorded and came back absolutely reeling. So she stayed home and began pouring through novels and entering appropriate quotes in the Excel file, for words such as *Excoriating, Ecstatic, Embroiled,* and *Evocative.* She was developing an almanac inside the encyclopedic spreadsheet of emotions.

Before long black and white wasn't enough. She began charting in colors. She saw that the red of eros could mix with the indigo of embarrassment for a feel of something like romantic chagrin. A sleepy blue over the wakingest yellow conjured up a quality of being enraptured—green. She understood *Endangered* from her empathy with elephants. She typed *Extinction*. That seemed the grayest of all emotions. But what could she do about this wrenching sensation? She could only enter information. And, eventually, edify. Her entries might even educate. It would take her an eternity to get all the emotions deeply felt and fully categorized in their colors. She was making a commitment for a lifetime at least.

When next her family gathered at the long, long table and popped the excruciating formal question one more time, "What endeavor entices you?" she, now the editor par excellence, was able to answer definitively: "*The Encyclopedia of Emotions.*" That's what her spreadsheets became—not an index, but a trove.

Eventually E did go out and experience every one of the emotions on her list, though she always returned to enfold among them, the family's eccentric, ever their own enigma, their brainy expert, their savant, a bit erratic, but increasingly enlightened, and always enlivening their esprit.

The Flibbertigibbet's Flaw

A flute would flare—then fifteen-year-old F would flounce onstage, positively fetching in her French-fashioned gown. Every night before she went on, two dressers would primp her: first the chemise, then the petticoats, last the farthingale under her skirts. Then they'd glue the thread-like cord of a microphone beneath her wig. F spent her mornings taking minuet classes so she could float across the boards in her furbelows. Every afternoon she ran her frivolous lines. Her speeches had to be measured to the forkful. Six nights and two afternoons a week she minced delicately through her role. The discipline!

F simply didn't have the personality of a flibbertigibbet. She had to tame her own full flavor in favor of the flirt she played. F was a free spirit—she itched at the fetters of fake frivolity. Yet she had fortitude. Under all the layers of frippery, she'd focus deeply on her performance, just as she practiced. But there were always one or two flaws. Every night she'd make a teensy mistake no one else would notice.

Except for one other person. The tall young flutist in the velvet jacket would notice. He was the musician who gave F her cues. He followed her with his flute through all the hours of lights and blocking and prancing in her finery. His flourishes on the silver keys prompted the words she tried so hard to say in the exact same order every time. He gave her fervor form. She was fire, but he was flow. He held her rhythms, careful not to destroy the fantasy of the audience.

And one night F performed flawlessly!

"Hey, I didn't eff up once!" she shouted backstage immediately after the final curtain, forgetting the audience, still in the theatre, forgetting the microphone, still taped under her wig. Her fugitive shout seemed to light the dark stage brighter than firelight, and it felt to her, in the blackness behind the curtain, that she was strangely falling—falling . . .

Immediately the flutist threw his silver instrument into its case and fled from the wings toward her, extending both his arms and flattening her to his chest, burying her nose against his breastbone through his jacket, fitting his delicate fingers over her mouth and rocking her back and forth like someone who had just burst into tears.

Only F had not. She had merely let fly the first un-rehearsed words she'd spoken since the start of rehearsals.

She thought she'd performed it all to a fare-thee-well! But she had flown to the feast of frankness too soon.

F felt like a cave girl. She could have been tearing seared flesh from bones with her teeth, smearing juices with the back of her hand across her flushed face far from the fetters of formal talk and dress.

How could she have freed herself so early—and done it so ferociously loud?

Now her mouth was muted by his fine hand. She smelled his wrist at the margin of his sleeve, and twisted toward the fragrance of his neck, his hair feathered at the edge of his collar, his foulard loosening . . . and she rose up into another kind of cave, the cave of the flutist's chest. Fiercely he tried to blow out that fire of hers, but he only fed it as he muffled her, muffled her, muffled her with a furred darkness where touch existed as the only sense except smell, the fog-smell of behind-the-curtain, and the palm-and-finger sheen-of-sweat intoxication as she fell against his velvet coat and he fell against the velvet curtain and they fell into the fanning of their fever.

Gallimaufry

Grab the pillowcase and go! Galumph down the stairs. Pass the growling chairs! Graze the grimacing table! Run the gauntlet of the hall, little g!

Even with his glasses on little g could hardly see the glimmer of sun at the end of the hall in the gloom. Everything was alive.

The clothes tree almost got him in its giant arms . . . But little g was nimble. He slid away, taking his loot out the screen door into a blast of summer.

After he plopped the pillowcase on the warm porch floor, he dropped into a squat. The floorboards shifted and wheezed in the heat. What ears little g had!—he heard everything. A glissade of bottle caps gushed from his pillowcase. Each cap had its own sound: screamy Cream Soda, crybaby Loganberry, giggle-bubble Ginger Ale. The bottle caps gyrated in the glow.

Back in the dark house Grandma packed his lunch. *Plunk.* Grapes and graham crackers plus a gooey sandwich hit the bottom. *Snap.* He heard the lunchbox clamp shut.

Little g lay down sideways, extending his arm. His quick fingers flipped each bottle cap to its topside. *Click, nick, tick, wick, pick!* He gathered and graded them. Some had giveaways printed under their tops. They got the top row. He kept the dented ones cooling in the bottle cap hospital—a rectangle of shade made by the porch banister.

As the sun warmed his knees and bum, little g looked backward, to curl around what he held. Grown *G*s always have to face goalward, but a quick little *g* can grab what glistens. He touched the smooth backs of the caps, learning not to get nicked by the sharp parts. Compared to the wee caps, he was Gargantua.

Grouping was little g's gift. He never tired of arranging his caps. Today he had them in Good, Great, Gold. He spied a squashed one and moved it to the bottle cap cemetery, a plastic bag. Light glanced off his glasses.

"Time to go!" gargled Grandma's voice from way inside the dark house.

Now he had to swoop them all into the case. Back through the gauntlet: the cave of gargoyle clocks and gewgaws, their garbled gibberish taunting him as he veered through the gloom to the kitchen where his hand glommed onto the handle of his lunchbox. Got it!

Goodbye!

Back again past the gnarling, gnashing Goliath of the

chesterfield, the gnomes of the unlit lamps galvanizing down the dark hall, lunchbox and pillowcase in hand, gesticulating to the day camp bus driver.

Wait!

Here comes the genius of the bottle caps, the Gulliver of Gleaners.

Hotel Religion

Half-pint h, the youngest in his family, slipped through the arms and legs of his huge older brothers as they hurtled around the house, snapping towels at one another—Mrs. H howling and Mr. H hectoring and growling. Nothing h had was his own; if it was his, the big guys swiped it. The little brother rarely had a towel to himself for eighteen years, let alone a pillow he could claim—they were all hurled in the fights. Diminutive, but big of heart, he longed for harmony.

Where was it? All the half-pint knew was that the battles got hairier as the brothers got huger. Mr. H grew humorless, and Mrs. H grew haggard.

Once a week, after Mrs. H got down on her hands and knees and cleaned the only bathroom, h charged in fast for a shower, watching the dirt from his toes swirl down the drain. Then he got to be first to use the navy blue towel that his mother said hid the grime.

Home became a dash between harrowing and hazarding.

The food fights took on guerilla tactics. The brothers and father faced off. The house became hell. h slipped out, forgotten. He hid and did his schoolwork on the laundry table in the basement, even spending the night draped across three plastic baskets of sweat pants when things upstairs got too hot.

Homework made h strangely happy: hypotenuses, hypotheses, hierarchies, horizontal vectors, heptagons, hexagons, and the breathtaking height of lines, especially if they were attached by a horizontal.

Upon high school graduation he left to dodge Heineken cans in hallowed halls and got a hard-won degree in hydraulic engineering.

At last H came to live in his own grownup habitat, a starter house where one bathroom spilled with his wife's girlie stuff and the other overflowed with his twins' disposable diapers. Plus, as a beginning specialist in floods, bridges, and sewage, H had a hectic new job—now he would travel for a living. His parents were no longer healthy and his brothers too busy brawling to care.

Harmony rested on a ledge between the heights of love's responsibilities.

As he packed for work in the next city, then kissed his wife and baby boys goodbye, a thought announced itself: *You need a religion.* He confirmed his reservation in the taxi, got on the plane, and before he ate his peanuts, the thought became his own: *I need a spiritual life.* Later, he slipped his roll-aboard into the complimentary van, and arrived at his hotel, a mighty fortress of towers with a horizontal marquee.

Hark! The bellmen heralded his welcome with to-ing and fro-ing. The wheels of the luggage cart sang a kind of hymn. He made his way to the reception desk, presided over by a man in a gray suit with a stand-up collar. *The altar,* H realized, *the holy place the visitor never gets to go behind.* Readily he signed the register—a certificate of confirmation—then signed his credit card for incidentals—a pledge of tithes.

Chandeliers hung from the vaulted ceiling. Humongous urns of hibiscus overflowed. The height and space were like a hemisphere of childhood, free and protected. Well, like the childhood he hoped his twins would have.

You don't need to bring a thing to a hotel, H marveled. *It's the respite every sinner from the street deserves.* (Not that H was much of a sinner.)

The hush of the carpet led him down a nave of a hall to his own heavy door. There, a king-size bed awaited him with at least six pillows, all his own. *For such is the mansion I enter,* H said to himself, plopping his overnight bag on the luggage rack and hanging up his coat.

White towels lined the marble and mirrored bathroom. *Hosanna!* Clean lines marked all his ablutions. He attended to his beard in the backlit makeup mirror. He lifted up his washcloth as if he were lifting his infant sons from the arms of his wife. Fear not. *Hallelujah!* Share not your blessings this once.

Refreshed, he strolled out to explore the offerings. At the hotel buffet a cantaloupe square dissolved on his tongue. At the rail of the bar he drank the hotel's wine. A telephone, like a saint in a niche, rang with his client's voice, confirming his morning appointment. The sacred music the elevator played was Mrs. H's favorite old song, "Heart and Soul".

That night, the service was room service. He ate in bed, then called his wife and heard the twins gurgle on the phone, turned out the light, and slept the sleep of the temporary hermit.

In the morning, he was called to wake. When he sauntered over to pee in the vast bathroom, bigger than his bedroom at home, the incense rose from tiny soaps. If not home, why not have a haven?

After he dressed, he called his wife, who said, "You sound so peaceful, honey." And as he placed a hefty tip in the small wicker collection basket on top of the mahogany chest of drawers, H noticed the hotel's evaluation checklist, printed on the heaviest card stock. Pressing characteristically hard on his pen, he wrote in block letters his one-word comment, "HEAVEN."

Doctor I and the Illustrator

It was independence itself she helped her patients aim for, though Dr. I expressed this indirectly. She vowed to ease the irrational, inspire the irritable, illumine the ill, and lead them all into images of themselves, pictures they could draw internally. Dr. I thought all her patients were intrepid, even the timid ones. She understood that ichors of being flowed up and down the cores of every last one of them.

Dr. I needed all her insight to deal with a new patient, the silent man. Intimidated, he sat on the beige couch for nearly forty minutes and did not speak. His back was curved. His posture was terrible. "I'm an illustrator," he said. "No words necessary." At the end of the session he pointed to her computer and said, "Check the website."

Before the second session Dr. I learned that he designed icons. Logos for companies.

"These icons are so imaginative," Dr. I marveled.

"Not really," he said, "just . . ."

"Just?"

"The image speaks."

After thirty-five minutes of *not* speaking he said, "My son passed away," and got up to leave.

Between the interstices of silence in the third session, Dr. I finally learned that the man had relocated to be with his son in his illness, and had in the process deeply connected with his grandson. The impetuous boy was a delight. But the mother just couldn't explain to the boy that his daddy had died. Thus it fell to the illustrator to do it. In despair he had conveyed the essentials to the boy through drawing.

It was not until the fourth session, when he brought Dr. I the black-and-white cartoons he'd used to illustrate for his grandson his son's exit from this world, that she discovered the man's presenting problem was not death, but life. It seemed his grandson now looked to him to perform an impossible fatherly task. The imp had volunteered the illustrator to speak to his school. Not just the class, but the whole elementary school. Impossible! Yet inescapable. The thought of it brought the silent man to his knees.

"It's why I'm here," he said to Dr. I. "Not about my son. My grandson."

Dr. I suggested biweekly appointments for a while. They marked their calendars. "What a chatterbox I've been," he concluded.

But the next time he did not come.

At first Dr. I was surprised. He hadn't seemed resistant, only quiet and monosyllabic.

She sat her in chair and waited. Dr. I did not just wait, though. She thought about him. She spent the hour with an invisible patient applying all her experience, and to a degree, her innocence, into thinking about him.

And the next time he did not come. Of all the actions she could take, she had to choose inaction; she had to wait. Therefore, Dr. I did not take off for a break at the coffee shop. She stayed in her chair. Inhabited it for this man. Is there such a thing as distance healing?

Or is it just time? Having to so severely structure her patience for her patient soon became a kind of irritation. Like an ink blot her irritation spread into her general thoughts about her profession. For instance, that tired, if true, insect image people use to describe becoming independent: that individuals would wriggle from helpless caterpillars into butterflies. Insipid, if accurate. But to her the transformation seemed more architectural. A column of a self, the *I* within each of those patients, needed to stand up, and then to lean into the storm of life.

The next week the man returned.

When she explained that she had kept each hour of his absence exclusively for him, thinking about him and his situation, he was incredulous. But moved. His head seemed to float up to the top of his spine.

It's tiring work, standing up for your self. You come from the ground up. And yet you do have wings. A little *i*-child flies about, but a grown *I* has had to take those wings inside.

Using her instincts, she repeated to him something he had said before to her. "The image speaks."

He left. But the next time he came back.

"I could show them something. Illustrate." For the silent man, it all came down to a gaggle of children wiggling on the floor of a gym waiting for him to say something.

The possibilities for what that might be intoxicated both of them. (Dr. I imagined she heard the sound of a once-rusty pump. Could it be drawing the ichors of existence through his veins?)

"A huge pad," the not-quite-as-silent man said. "An easel."

At the appointed time of the assembly, he brought to the school a tall easel with a gigantic flip pad. From all the other kids, he selected his grandson to come to the front. He asked him a few questions, the same way he inquired of his clients at work, and then, as the boy directed, he drew an icon for him in response: a little-kid coat of arms with an insect theme. The man fashioned it with a caterpillar and a butterfly. Something all the kids could try for themselves.

Needless to say, all the children wanted him to create an icon for them. He relented, but now he was only on the fourteenth of his 341st flying-insect coat of arms.

Dr. I learned this, in detail, as the man cartooned the event for her the following week. "You ignited their imaginations!" she said.

Yes, he was surprised how much they'd liked it.

"I got inspired," the man told Dr. I.

And so he shielded their inkling hearts.

While Jiggle Juggles, J Makes Jam

 When you've been jilted, judged, jeered at, and japed at by a jealous jerk who's put your self-confidence in jeopardy by going for your jugular, you can always make jam, as J in desperation did.

She bought ripe oranges for the marmalade, perfect spheres. She was jaded, joked at, jolted into life alone—again. Her little daughter Jiggle jumped around the house in her striped jammies, jitterbugging here and there in a world of her own.

J peeled the oranges and measured the sugar and set the huge pot to boil. As J made jam, Jiggle was a jack-in-the-box, a one-girl jamboree. Jiggle was all beginning—she was January. She was all bloom. She was June, she was July.

For every bit of the mother's jaundice, the daughter was jonquil.

When you have suffered from jeremiads and jactations, you can always line up jars and boil them in the canning pot as the marmalade bubbles and your hair sticks in

sugary tendrils to your temples—and, out of the corner of your eye, watch a jimsonweed of a girl doing a jig, her jelly belly bobbling. Through the jungle of recriminations and blame for the jackass who walked away, Jiggle brought J the scent of jasmine.

The girl took the three extra oranges and started to juggle, just like they taught in gym. She chanted the words of the instructions as she did it:

One ball eye-level, elbows in.
Two balls, up, up, catch, catch.
Then the third: criss-cross applesauce.
Just let one drop.

"Don't throw ahead of you," she warned herself as she picked up the bruised oranges.

Jiggle was on a junket.

But J was on her journey.

The marmalade bubbled, the hot jars joggled, and J reached in with her tongs to remove and turn them onto the fresh dish towels on the counter. She jiggered her jam funnel into the jars, poured the marmalade, and used her magnet wand to fish out the metal tops from the simmering water and pop them on the jars in a jiffy.

Then she sat down in the quiet joy of a job completed and watched Jiggle juggle.

Why justify? J thought. *Why joust with a jackass? Be jovial!*

Well, she wasn't quite to the outright jovial stage, but a jot of *joie de vivre* had returned with the popping of the lids on the marmalade jars. Some of her old juice.

A Knight's Knack

 Kid K thought he had it all in hand. The brash knight-errant charged his mount from crusade to crusade. He held the reins, got the kudos—and kanoodled with all the princesses. Knightlife was a tournament!

Young K started his career so long ago that knight was actually pronounced *k-nick-t*. His loyal squire called him "a parfit valiant k-nick-t." Kid K was certainly brave, right down to his very kidneys. But he was also a bit of a k-nucklehead. He could handle a steed with silvery ease, or kiss a lady holding back her hair, but kindness with words wasn't his long suit. "Son of a bawd!" "Beggar!" He said the first thing that came to his mind, uncensored. "Filthy-stockinged coward!" "Heir of a mongrel!" "K-nife-nosed k-nave!"

Then came the accident . . .

Don't look!

Yes . . . it involved an ax.

Yes . . . it was gruesome.

Oh, close your eyes to the bloody hand in the dust, the fingers sticking out . . .

(But every time we write a *k*, we still sketch a ghost of his fingers protruding from his severed knightly hand.) It was his right hand, the rein-holder. His love hand. The loss made him want to lie down and die.

When his squire brought him breakfast, he said *kNo*, and then *kNo* to his trusty steed and *kNo* to his classy suit of armor and *kNo* to kissing every one of his grieving amours. His thoughts, which he never paid much attention to anyway, simply came to a stop. Dropped, just like the *k* that was beginning to loosen from the very word that defined him.

"Kill me!" he implored his squire, but the loyal man refused.

"Kill me!" the k-nick-t insisted. "I'm a lily-livered rogue, I'm a filthy-gloved coward. I'm a beggar and a k-nave." None of this was true, his faithful servant knew, except for the fact that K wore a very disreputable looking mitten-bandage over his wrist. He thought he was a coward because he was crying, but his old squire saw the kernel of a different bravery.

He sewed his liege two special gauntlets, one for his left hand, one for his right arm, all stitched with seed pearls, one for every tear K had shed.

"You mayn't continue to joust, milord," the squire ventured, "but there are things you can still do single-handedly."

K regarded the gloves with wet eyes. *Did he really want to die?*

"Try them on, my liege."

The minute K donned the seed-pearled gauntlets, the *k* in the word *knight* clanked to the ground, its sound disappearing. Without the premature clatter of his first letter, K's thoughts became attempts. He essayed. *I'm still kicking,* he told himself.

Stronger, if slower, his thoughts slid from one another. *To imitate a rare true-penny is my aim,* he decided.

As his thoughts became stately and deep, his talk slowed. *A honey-tongued gallant may I become,* he resolved. And he found that it was easier to listen to others. *Well-wishing, best-tempered, lion-booted may I be.*

How to live became his mission. But unlike most philosophers, K didn't live entirely in his head. He was sharply aware of his body. Every time he picked up a knife and held an apple close to his chest to peel the red skin, he valued what he had—and lived in a certain amount of fear that he'd lose his other hand. *"Oh, precious sweet-suggesting valentine of mine,"* he crooned.

He came to understand that how to live meant how to go on. Decades passed. The former knucklehead became a man with a knack. In time, knack grew to know-how.

Eventually he outlived his contemporaries. Then he outlived reigns and generations. Castles crumbled. Dray horses became thoroughbreds. Thoroughbreds became automobiles. Royalty became Hollywood. And he remained, a silent-*k*'d knight, remarkably fit, still using his same suit of armor, his pearly gloves, still quickly dropping on bended knee to a lady (and deft at removing her knickers single-handedly).

One day, when asked for his philosophy by his new squire, K said, "Smooth-faced celestial well-wishing." And at the new squire's stymied look, the knight amplified, "Cuckoo-budded compassion." His old squire, the glove maker, had centuries ago passed on, and many attendants had come and gone, and now this squire was a mystified personal assistant in flip-flops. K tried again to help out his new young squire PA: "My philosophy is . . . " The knight was going to say that it was "Wafer-caked best-temper and song," but realized that if he really had an attitude of wafer-caked best-temper, he would simplify for the boy.

"Kindness."

L at Her Pool

 L was lazing in a chaise by her pool when she heard a languid voice behind her. She was startled, but the lush baritone was so assured she didn't immediately turn around. Instead, she stayed poised in her white retro swimsuit and let the voice envelop her like a cloak.

You've done a lot for Hollywood film, it said. *You'll be remembered, just as your mother was.* To say L was at a lull in her career was a laughable understatement. She had been all but forgotten. But that compliment lifted her up. That was what a compliment did, made you look at yourself afresh. She blushed a bit, then looked down at her toes.

Lovely swimsuit. I like the retro look with the red toenails. Who was this Lancelot?

Her hand went automatically to her hair, and she pulled at her curls. It was the same gesture she'd made since she was five years old, while tugging at her mother's silk robe with the fur trim.

When L turned around at last, she found the flatterer's face was hidden beneath a mask and hat. Was that a hint of a pencil mustache below the shadow of the brim? He wore a long black satin cape with a crimson lining, and he smelled of musk and lust and . . . *it couldn't be* . . . a distinct whiff of lily-of-the-valley. After a moment of staring, L's eyes locked with the eyes that might be behind the brim and the mask.

Then with disappointment and surprise she watched him turn away, beginning to disappear through the striped canvas walls of her poolside cabana. At the very end, his cape snagged on the cabana pole, and as he turned to urge it back with him, he knocked his hat askew. In seconds he vanished entirely.

Was he real? Oh yes, there at the tiled edge of the pool lay his leather mask. He must have lost it in those last seconds of his exit.

L laughed the iconic, laconic laugh that had made her famous, a second-generation, but no less luminous, movie star than her mother Miss Lily Valley had been. *Time to let go of vanity and get to the hospital,* she whispered to herself. She really had no time for a phantom lover.

When she rose from the chaise, she swooped up the mask. Later she deposited it at the back of her lingerie drawer, enjoying for a moment the creased leather amidst her lacy frou-frous. Then she forgot all about it in the rush to her husband's side.

Her third husband, the one she adored, was desperately ill. The first two were troublesome necessities, but this third . . . he was a kind of luxury at the end of her fulsome career. A career she had left for him. As she worked for his wellness, she realized with shock that laurels, even lustrous ones, don't last.

L's mother, Miss Lily Valley, had been a child star in the early talkies, a legendary girl with full, dark bangs, whose career lasted till she was nearly eighteen. Then she retired to have a family. But L, as an adult, had walked out on glamour for a newly chosen role—to give the love of her life all she herself had received: compliments. At first she was like a woman with a fortune so large she could give vast quantities away every day. Compliments? Lifeblood! She had banks of them. She knew how they fueled life. The admired thrive.

But her failing husband could not return her compliments. He was turned toward the next life, and compliments come only from this life. As he faced the shadows of the future, he forgot sweet-talk.

L seized her role. She complimented him on everything: his liver, his lymph, his lungs, his LDL cholesterol, his leucocytes, his limbs, his limbic system. She knew she had depleted her fortune of tributes, but she didn't care. In the matter of life and death, she tore the leaves off every laurel and pressed them to his forehead.

Under her ministrations he lingered—but at last her crooned litany had no effect. He passed into the next world.

Afterwards, time lounged on. L lowered her pace. She had no choice. The cameras had long passed her by. Yet even with all the time in the world to practice, she could not learn to compliment herself. She tried. But trying was faking it.

Ruefully she discovered the lesson of the compliment: like light through a lens, praise had to come from the outside in.

One day as she lay on the solitary chaise at her pool, L suddenly smelled lily-of-the-valley, and beneath it the scent of musk and leather.

Milady, I've come back for my mask, her ghost Lothario said, as if only sixty seconds had passed, not three times sixty weeks. Loose, limber, there he was, the glare of the sunshine behind that hat obscuring his face. His cape flapped its crimson silk interior. He lifted one leather-booted leg and leaned onto the chaise, his shadow enveloping her.

"How do you know I have it, milord?" she asked. *I know.* Well, of course he did. She got up and was about to saunter casually to her bedroom closet as if she were on camera. But she stopped.

"The price of the return," she said languorously to him, "is a look at your face." Lickety-split, he bowed his head.

Suddenly, he was all hat, and L was superstitiously unable to lift the brim. Instead she reached beneath and felt the thick hair of his full bangs.

Slowly she tipped the brim to reveal the lower part of his face. Yes, the pencil mustache was there. The lips were wide with a quirk of a smile. She anticipated that his eyes would be dark as forests. Yet as she pushed the brim fully back, his masculine visage disappeared. In its place loomed the luminous face of a child.

It was her mother as a tomboy with thick straight bangs and shining eyes. Somehow Miss Lily Valley was inside the Lothario.

Compliments tell you what you are. They tell you what you already know, but when other people know it, too, the lake inside you deepens. *You reflect them in your waters*, L thought, *and they reflect you in their eyes.*

When L was a precocious teenager, she once shouted at her mother, "That's narcissism!" as the retired actress reposed in satin at a dressing room mirror, recounting her compliments.

"No, darling," Lily said to her daughter. "Narcissism is craving your own reflection. A compliment is a response to one's effort at being."

Now L's phantom repositioned his mask and his mustache rematerialized. Through the mask, his eyes were liquid. He loitered a little, loath to leave, and she lolled on the chaise, watching him adjust his hat, then disassemble his cells into a vapor that passed through the cabana stripes with a pleasant hiss. A hint of *Muguet* hung in the air.

I need you even now, she thought, *even now.*

All around the pool the privet hedge enclosed a lustrous emptiness. So often the satin of our mother's glamour reincarnates itself as the shadow of amour. In the stillness where her ache for love almost echoed she plucked at her curls as she had as a child.

Time to highlight my locks and lacquer my nails, she thought, reaching for the poolside phone, hearing Miss Lily's lavish voice inside her own, leaving the phantom lover to evanesce into his next act. He did not return.

L had a next act, too. She did return to the screen, a splendid lady in a daring cameo, and she lived on the compliments she got for a long, long time.

M's Dream House

M loved the little house she shared with her mum, its magnolias and mansard roof. Inside, the smell of molasses and ginger had sunk into the timbers. Water mumbled from a hand pump, not a faucet tap. Music murmured, not from a radio, but from a soft piano. All was washed to softness—the sheets, the table linens. Even the gold rims on the old dishes were brushed down to a blur.

M had been a surprise late baby, and her mother was almost the age of a grandmother. There were only the two of them—plus Maugie, their cat.

M grew up thinking she understood her mum. But in fact she only understood her in daylight. The night world was where mum paced with her mountains of money worries. Down the hall M blissfully slept, and down in the basement Maugie moused, bringing her prizes up to the landing so M and Mum could find them first thing in the morning.

And in that morning light Mum's money misery vanished. She never spoke of it. But when Mum got sick, her worries magnified. Her illness brought the night world to daylight, though she still managed to hide it from her daughter. Mum could no longer hope for a miracle. Unbeknownst to M, just before Mum died, the ancient lady up and took misfortune into her own misguided hands. She sold their home to the neighbors who had always coveted it.

Why didn't she tell me? M plagued herself with questions all through the small funeral—she and her mum were the last of their line—and said to her distant cousins and her friends: *She never ever mentioned money*! Lawyers, real estate agents, and the neighbors of course were summoned. But the deal was done. Though M harbored murder in her heart for those greedy neighbors, she couldn't get the house back.

It's all MY fault—I should have known, M moaned.

It took a long time for her to settle these affairs. She'd taken a leave from her job at the museum, but eventually she had to go back to work. She and Maugie went to the only place M could afford to buy, a small but gleaming condominium. How could she transfer doilies and dusty velvet couches with broken legs into this glare? What was home any more? She had an iron bedstead, not a sleek futon. Of course Maugie kept finding her way back to the old homestead, and M had to keep quashing the mayhem in her heart as she retrieved the crafty little animal from that basement now full of the neighbor's traps instead of mice.

Up in the condo, M's dreams began. Each night she dreamed of a ruined house. Mornings she woke to a smell

m

like something left in an oven too long, a whiff of burnt molasses. Sometimes in a dream a window without a wall fell to the ground in mockery. Night after night in her sleep M shouldered mountains of blame. But then came morning.

All she could do was embrace the day. With her long shapely arms, she put on her makeup, donned her mackintosh, and struck out for the museum, determined to muddle through.

"It's not my fault, I know," she said to McM, the man who occupied the next desk. "I just miss my home." He offered her a meatloaf sandwich. She said, "I never knew my mum, after all." M's dreams went on mortgaging her nights. When she startled awake, there was only Maugie at the foot of the iron bedstead squeaking an unsatisfactory plastic rodent, and a monstrous stink of burnt molasses and cat pee.

M decided to bake. Using her mother's measuring cups, she chased the aftermaths of the dreams away by spicing the smells. With cinnamon, with allspice, with vanilla and cardamom, she made muffins, mousse, and meringues in the open-concept kitchen. She used all her mother's bowls, and all her mother's spoons, to expunge the smells—and she almost did.

Meanwhile, Maugie knew whenever workmen propped open a staircase door. The cat would slip into the hall, then escape down the stairwell through the service door. And M would get a call at the museum from the mingy mean-spirited neighbors.

"And what am I going to do with Maugie?" M moaned to McM.

"Your cat is lonely," he said. "Does she have service potential?"

Maugie would be tested. McM agreed to help.

The minute McM walked into the combo of gleam and old wood and velvet and iron, the marvelous smells wrapped around him. "You've been baking," he murmured approvingly, "in your farmhouse in the sky." But M was busy wrangling Maugie into the carrier.

Shortly the cat was deposited on the welcoming laps of ancient ladies in wheelchairs. That champion purr eased the ladies' hearts. Maugie aced the test. Seeing the ladies, something in M eased, too.

"My mother is a mystery I may never solve," she said to McM on one of their lunchtime trips to the old ladies. Maugie now went willingly into her carrier.

And so the bright weekday activities wore down the mountains of dreams. Blame became a molehill. M's nightmares became so predictable they were almost friendly. Metamorphosis set in. McM lingered when he held M's coat, and she lingered as he slipped it on. Their hands met when they put the cat carrier into the car. But these were the gestures of daylight.

Thinking she was ready to brave the evening light, M had made the mistake of inviting McM for Saturday dinner. When the day came, she lay in bed with a fever, vacuuming was abandoned, her mahogany hair unwashed. Though the mushroom soup gurgled on the stove and the mousse slept in the fridge, the main course had never been started. She left a message canceling.

McM arrived anyway with merlot and magnolias. He merged into M's mess. It smelled of cough drops and kitty litter and dust and the fragrance of a woman in a slept-in nightgown. She slid beneath layers of consciousness like the layers of the blankets he straightened for her. And then balancing two hot toddies, fully clothed, he climbed into the bed. Maugie obliged him with a space.

M was too weak to protest. She woke and drank and woke and slept. At midnight M sat up and slurped the mushroom soup held by McM. Magnificent . . .

And then she sank. That night of course she dreamed of a house, but this house was merely old, not ruined. It was the homestead, magnolias laden, sheet music still in the piano bench. When she woke, she smelled McM, still fully clothed at her side, his glasses on the floor, batted about by Maugie. Nothing smelled burnt. Unlike her mother, M didn't believe in miracles. She believed in muddling through. Slowly something had risen in her, like those moons you sometimes see in an afternoon sky, night inside the persistence of day. M sat up in bed, hugging her knees, looking at McM sprawled beside her. *The house at last is inside me*, she thought. *I've finally moved.*

The Negativo Trio

No was a violin, Not a viola, and Never a cello. They were noble instruments, but highly nonconformist. Prickly in personality, if sexy. Wayward. Always went in their own direction. Made odd choices. Loved the difficult. Naysayed the popular. Collectively unified in a single reaction to the mainstream: negative.

When they first chanced to come together, they doubted they would ever meld.

But the minute they began to make music, they discovered a numinous core to their triangle. They couldn't see this core, smell it, or touch it—and neither could their slender audience (thirty people on folding chairs in a church). But all felt it was a natural union of sound, nimble and sublime.

That night they became the Negativo Trio.

Retiring to nestle in the velvet warmth of their cases, they whispered to each other, debriefing and musing in the first of many nightly pajama parties. This very first evening they discovered that what they wanted above all were two things. One was to play their music with the very nacre of its nature, and the other was fame.

Night after night they played. Increased their bookings. Recorded. And were downloaded. They raised money to pay off the debt of their obscure choices. On stage they each shone with the patina of centuries: maple, spruce, and willow with an elegant varnish of gum arabic, honey, and the whites of eggs.

But they weren't famous, even though they played a nocturne as if every note were a black pearl.

Yet No, Not and Never did everything everyone advised them to *be* famous: they networked, they nodded nicely to publicists, they flashed their Negativo news on social media. But the fact was, the trio wasn't for everybody.

"Do you think it's our name?" Not the Viola asked. "Would we be more famous as the Nightingale Trio?"

"Nope," said Never the Cello. "Negativo has our *brio*." And Never was right. The three of them played with nerve. The knottier the piece, the better. They made their audiences reach.

"We should be sexier," No the Violin said. "Naughtier. It's our propensity for the minor key; we should lighten it up." But when they played in the minor key, their audiences felt they had arrived at the navel of the universe. The instruments could never give up the minor.

Would the Negativos ever learn what the people in the seats knew? The trio wasn't famous because, well, they kind of unnerved people. You had to have nettle to take them on.

Though they certainly wouldn't have said no to notoriety, eventually they had to admit that they could not surrender their quirks.

"We will never be famous," NEVER said one night after they had nestled in their cases for their midnight debriefing.

"I'm nauseous," said NO extravagantly.

"And neglected," said NOT excessively.

"Never," said NEVER decisively.

They would never fill the biggest halls. Or be the first name on the tips of tongues. And with the inverted logic of misplaced dreams, even though they had toured, had notched up reviews, and had triumphs and fans, and websites and bloggers, and a body of criticism devoted to them, they felt they had reached their nadir.

The next morning they couldn't seem to get up. They lay immobile, as if their velvet-lined cases were coffins.

A netherworldly silence descended.

The dust of despair drifted through the crack between the case tops and bottoms onto these living dead.

Time dragged like a dirty hem.

Naught into Nil.

Desolation into Dormancy.

Dormancy into . . .

                . . . Rest.

Rest into Snoozing.

Snoozing into Sleep.

Sleep into Healing.

The nostrum of sleep lasted until the pinkish light that heralds spring.

A noisy nuthatch drilled for insects in a nearby tree. It was a forest sound, yodel-y and ebullient. It awoke the maple and spruce and willow of the Negativo's constitutions. Their bodies couldn't help responding to the vernal signal given when spring utters its only word: *Nevertheless.*

If not fame, nevertheless music.

"Numbskull nuthatch!" NEVER growled.

"Ninny nuthatch," No yawned.

"Bumptious bird," NoT shifted, inadvertently jostling the snap to the dusty case. It sprang open. No unclicked and climbed out, too. And NEVER heaved the lid.

They played immediately of course, trying a violin piece by the underrated Nardini. Most thought him a lightweight, but the Negativos gave it their signature interpretation of naked necessity.

"Oh it was NOTHING," they began to say to one another as they did musical favors for themselves, producing scores of synchronicities and the occasional juicy nihilistic dissonance. They buoyed on their notes, as if a midnight Pacific of calm, rich, dark negatives were effused with luminescence.

How relieved their listeners were to have them back. Again their audiences were made aware of the noses between their ears. That slight, brief piquancy in the nostrils was the smell of earthly harmony. It came from within the airy column that united the instruments, the nucleus of their refusal to suit. Such accord, though it is as rare as ease, seems like nothing.

And so the Negativo Trio was known as a trio's trio.

Not famous, but known.

Contrary to the vicissitudes of fame, ease is the path of the known, smooth as the satin of the instruments' finish. To be recognized, yet not to suffer the disadvantages of fame, is a state so ideal it is the pinnacle of a career. No, Not and Never had at last woken up to that.

O's Full Circle

When it came time for O to horrify her parents, she dated lassos, loops of rope who threw themselves around her opulent waist (how they knew where it was, even she had no idea), and pulled her tight, clenching her in the middle. But an *0* roped in the midriff becomes two smaller *0*s—an *8*. She knew that she wasn't a number.

She was a realization, a shock, a unity.

Still, she loved being squeezed by the lassos because then at least she had some definition, a way to fit into someone . . .

"But you're our little opal, complete in yourself!" the outraged senior Os objected. Objurgate her as they did, their daughter took every occasion to offend them, hugged in two so often by the lassos that she had little waist-dents in her sides. Each time she thought, *Now someone can hold me, and we can sweetly osculate*! But within a few hours she had plummed back into perfection.

"We're earning a zero in parenting," Daddy-O said to Mom.

Onward went their family operetta, the adult Os overreacting and the teen provoking, till late one night in the kitchen after Mom had retired to bed, Daddy-O said softly to his daughter, "When you came into this world, you were a lovely little ochre dot, you were the blink of an eye. You were just perfect . . . "

At that O was desolate.

Complete she might be, but she felt incomplete—for how could she ever conjoin? "I wish I were still a dot," was all she said to Daddy-O, and then went up to bed.

There she fell into pessimism. Was anything worth doing?

For the rest of her senior year she lay, otiose, on an ottoman. Nightly the Os discussed the situation. For them, the state of an *0* was sublime. *0*s opened doors, created occasions and, best of all, offered opportunities! Why was their daughter so mopingly hopeless when the natural state of an *0* is optimism?

Young O fulfilled her obligations and graduated, rolling across the stage to get her diploma like everyone else, if not with aplomb, at least with a forward motion.

On she went to university. There she became a bio major, deciding to orbit solo for a while, achieving her orgasms as a unity unto herself.

One day after the lecture on *ovipara* (her favorite animals, the egg-layers), something brushed against her at the lab table. "I'm assigned to share this station, too," whispered a lanky, elongated oval. "I just transferred in."

She looked into his long, transparent center.

"What's your name," he asked her.

O frowned. She'd really been hoping to keep this lab table all to herself. "I'm O," she said.

"A letter *0*," he smiled as he began to set up his half of the station. "I do revere the capacities of letters." He jiggled the oxygen source, "Hey, does this work?" She showed him how to unstick the lever. "Thanks. My name is Zero, since you didn't ask."

Something began to oscillate.

"A number," she said. "In high school I tried to become a number."

"What did you want to do that for?" 0 asked her. "*0* is the word of poets! O rapture, O divine."

"O shit, O hell, O damn," she reminded him.

During 0's enthusiastic and O's reluctant cooperation in the lab assignment, by chance he brushed against her again. It was the farthest thing from a lasso that she could imagine, but there was something . . . a valence exchange . . . like static from a balloon. He did give out a dreamy scent of stretched rubber.

"Zeros," he said when they signed off their experiment, "consume a huge amount of energy. Want to go for an all-day breakfast?"

In the booth of the coffee shop, they had the first of many intense, overwhelming conversations.

"But the price of being a universe unto yourself is solitude," O said, "isn't it?"

"Even perfection needs company," 0 said casually, tucking into the oatmeal he'd ordered as an appetizer before his omelet arrived.

She had met a positive thinker. Slowly she chewed her onion bagel.

"*0* is what everyone in every language says when they're overwhelmed. *You* give them the syllable to say. You're the world!" he said between bites.

She was amazed at his bottomless capacity.

"Me," he continued, "I'm the perfect absence. I'm the last. And the first." After he polished off the oatmeal and the omelet, he ordered the Old-Fashioned Pancakes, which he insisted she share.

A mandorla of optimism began to surround her.

"I'm dating a zero!" she texted Mom and Daddy-O. On the phone she told them, "He's thrillingly airy inside and clear."

"What joy!" they said. A zero was a zillion times better than a lasso.

0 had the lightest of touches, tender, every contact a whisper from his nothingness to her being. It was not a

matter of fitting. It was a matter of melodious proximity. Like two balloons inflated to perfect shape, they float-bumped, kissing at every opportunity. And as they lightly collided under the covers in her dormitory room, they entered the oomph of omphalos—an uroborian circle where O came into her own.

The Poet

As P strolled the path around the pond, he sniffed the humid air. His kimono brushed the parched ground. The metals of the earth rose up in traces of dust and hints of lightning: a waft of petrichor, the smell before the rain.

Beyond the pale hills of his peaceful land, scores of horse soldiers prepared their armor. Soon the soldiers would sweep across the plains, and the dry politics of princely maneuverings would be as rice paper soaked with blood. Instead of petty policies—immensity. Peaceful farmers would be impaled, paltry officials imprisoned—twisted, screaming, then praying. There on the dusty path the young poet P was just perceiving the beforeness of it all, the *pre-*.

From his masters he had learned that immensity makes the small crucial. A little poem before a big war becomes a necessity.

And like a small poem on a long scroll, a lily pad appeared on the pond. P stopped to peer. He puzzled through its pattern of green inside green on water.

A poem began to perfuse. It was inside P, but it was also on the lily pad.

At . . . On . . . At first only prepositions came to him.

He stared into the water, seeing the silvery clouds reflected. Then he leaned at an extreme angle and noticed the pattern of his gown wavering in the reeds. A pinpoint of a poem stabbed him, like the sharp scent of earth before the rain. Petrichor: *before, before.*

Then drops pelted the pond, pipped at the pond, plunged toward it, plummeted into it, driving P to take refuge beneath the deep tiled eaves of his house.

Inside the sliding paper doors were a desk and a futon. On the desk lay a brush. On the futon lay a lover in uneasy sleep on petal-printed silk.

He chose the desk. He lifted the brush while looking down at the restive slumberer. In a mere matter of stopped time he had his poem, written from the very tissues of an arm and hand that could plunge a sword.

Silver soldiers mass
on far horizons, but here,
silk pools on the bed.

The rain rained; moisture curled the edges of the paper. Seventeen syllables, an epic of energy, made him drowsy and hungry. His lover still asleep, he rose, ate leftover peaches poached in soy sauce and ginger, and, with the rain a

drizzle, thought again of his poem. How could he have loved it in the instant after he wrote it, but now be so unsure?

He sat at his desk again. Another one? This time he drafted:

Poppy? Penis up.
Prow into periwinkle.
Peony behind.

After he calligraphed the puzzle of passion across the page, he woke the one in the pond of pink silk, and they proved it on the futon. He heard the pluvial patter on the eaves, while they angled and slipped, perspiring on silk. The stamping and snorting of the horses sweating in their armor was far too far away to be sensed by P, but he heard. He felt the pond muddied and the roof cracked and the poems scattered. How far was he now from this picture in his mind? He worked to make his pleasure stay, pitiable and small against the portents rising, for P was afraid this afternoon would never be remembered after the bloody conquering.

But later the barbarians would bivouac in this house, the pond saved for drinking water, the path roughened by horses, and the reverse of P's scroll used for another man's military diary, his afternoon's foreboding and pleasure a preparation for the future, and in the future, a stay against another's view of the past.

Q's Quest

 Some quests begin before a person ever learns to walk. Q's began at the foundling home, when he was still in diapers. They'd kept anything pointed from the Quonset hut where they housed the orphaned newbies, and later the house mothers forbade the children all but scissors with round edges, even table knives.

"Mind, now stay in the queue," they said, when his fingers reached for a safety pin or a paring knife or, once, one of the razors they kept (usually under lock and key) for the older boys. Q slipped back in line.

Only the blunt was available to him, nothing to question, naught with an edge. Best pretend to be dull (though that was hard with a high IQ) and never query:

Why hide the scissors? Why hide the razor? Why speak so sharply? Why no mums? No dads? At night in his bed, listening to the breathing of all the other boys in the long room, he also asked himself, *Why me?*

When the house mothers changed shifts, there were always some unsupervised minutes, and that's when the boys sprang into swashbuckling. Q loved leaping from bed to bed with an imaginary sword in hand. *En garde!*

At sixteen, with a razor cut on his chin from the new trial of shaving himself, Q stood at the doors of the Royal Flower Hall. He was quaking. This was the very first day of work in his life. He'd been supposed to be a shop assistant, a quotidian job like those of the other orphans who were all sent out to live as apprentices—to return only if found unsuitable. However, the Royal Flower Keeper had stepped in and demanded to know the name of the boy meant to be sent to the local florist, and now young Q was called to prep flowers for the Queen.

"Can't someone else do it?" He quailed as the Flower Keeper handed him a quilloned silver thorn knife. Q didn't want to be found unsuitable.

He quivered as thousands of roses arrived—he was supposed to separate their long, tangled stems, cut off the thorns, and queue them up straight on the tables for the arrangers.

"But I'm new!" Q cried. He couldn't quell his horror at the prospect of lifting a real blade to cut the thorns.

"Look, dear, no quibbling. If you work here, you're qualified," the Flower Keeper said. Her knuckles bloomed out of the crooked stems of her hands. "Hold the knife with two fingers behind this little crossbar, that's the quillon, and snip under the thorn."

She did it with elegant speed. One thorn gone.

"It's like swordsmanship," the Flower Keeper joked, wielding her knife, fencing in miniature mime. In Q's head rang the orders of the house mothers, "DON'T TOUCH!" But in his fingers lay his imaginary weapon come alive.

"No time to be quiescent," she said. "Equipoise is all."

Don't quit now, Q said to himself. If he quit, he'd have to slink back to the orphanage, a failed apprentice, instead of going home to his newly found haven, a cold-water flat with a coin-operated heater, all his own. There he'd store the new paring knife his paycheque would buy, the pointed scissors . . . So Q quashed his fear and set to work.

He began to duel through the roses.

"*En garde!*" he whispered, lunging toward his petaled quarry.

Soon there were thorns everywhere (some a bit bloody), but he did not make any big mistakes. He wasn't perfect, like the Flower Keeper, but he was catching on. Like quicksilver she flashed her knife, each stem quickening with the sharpest cut.

Instinctively Q used the quartata maneuver, a quarter turn to the inside, protecting himself as he flicked each thorn into the quagmire of floral detritus on the floor. With each toss of the thorn he added to what appeared to the Flower Keeper to be his nascent gift.

As the lorries loaded with rose baskets and vases and bowls roared off to the palace, he quietly pocketed a thorn.

Then the first question he'd ever spoken aloud curlicued to his lips. And because he'd had to save up this query for sixteen years, he posed the essential one, previously mouthed only to himself at night in bed:

Why?

"Pourquoi?" said the Flower Keeper. "For the Equerry, of course. And he for the Queen. You know who *she* is."

"Just a flower of a figurehead," Q quipped.

The boy's quick-witted, the Flower Keeper thought, and said, "We'll require you tomorrow."

And for quadruple tomorrows after that and after that, until Q began to accumulate expertise. Know-how defines a person, especially someone who's grown up watching his *P*s and *Q*s. He no longer quavered, quadrillions of roses now quasi-ordinary, royal waste a quiddity.

I'm not a quitter, he'd said to himself, and each night went back to his cold-water flat where he had enshrined that little thorn in a matchbox.

Well, he didn't live in a cold-water flat now. Now he lived in a sunlit house with a stash of razors in the marble bathroom and, in the drawers of his magnificent kitchen, a motherlode of paring knives, bread knives, steak knives, bird's beak parers, boning knives, cheese knives, chef's, clam, and carving knives, filleters and mincers.

Now Q was Senior Keeper of the Royal Flower Hall, walking across a stage toward the Queen herself. He had kept the talisman thorn from his very first day with the roses. Just that afternoon he had taken it out and dropped it in the pocket of his tuxedo, anticipating touching it for luck before he received his award from Her Majesty.

But when the Queen posed her standard question, "Have you come a long way?" Q was quite bewildered as to how to answer.

Sometimes a simple question cuts into an aromatic world of mysteries. But we must learn to answer, to cut. Q, his distinguished silver hair perfectly trimmed, his neck properly shaved, looked down at the curls on the Queen's forehead and remembered his first unspoken word, *Why.*

A quixotic word, an essential thorn. It had pricked him awake, into manhood.

Arrangements of roses passed through his mind—how those magnificats of magentas quenched his imagination. How the choral crooning of pale pinks calmed his qualms. Among roses he had reached his quintessence.

Yet, is it a large enough life, to arrange roses for a Queen? When the whole world out there hurtled toward famine and war? He hadn't intended to stay, to make a future in flowers, taking people's breath away with something so spectacularly unnecessary as his rose floats. He had been a thorn in someone's side, spectacularly unnecessary himself. He'd been sent out into the world alone, blunted by the unknown facts of his identity—his search for his parents rewarded only by locked doors, locked cabinets and, later, graveyards.

Patiently Her Majesty waited for his answer. In physical distance he had come a short way, but he'd swashbuckled miles to reach the end of his quest.

"Only from Kew Gardens, Your Highness," Q answered simply at last.

Then she put into his palm the royal thank-you, in a quilted sleeve: a silver rose wreath made from an ancient mold that gave it stylized petals, prickly leaves and, cut in at the bottom of the circle, a thorn.

R and her Great Egret

 R had loved reversible images ever since she saw her first optical illusion. It was hanging on the wall of the art room in her small island school: the duck that was also a rabbit. R regarded the bird reversing into the mammal and the mammal reversing into the bird every time she went to art class. She loved drawing animals with her crayon lines.

When she was older, she discovered the famous white vase that reversed to two black profile silhouettes—a roller-coaster ride for her eyes. And the illusion that most resisted her perception was the one of a young woman in a hat that became an old woman in furs.

R was surprised to encounter the baffling drawing in tatters on the office wall of the pithy, rumpled, renowned ecology professor, head of the Nature Centre where she applied to intern. The ramshackle field station sat on a rise at the edge of the wetlands, home to those magnificent fishers, the great egrets. She was determined to learn to draw their round white bodies and black stalky legs. The professor saw she was rigorous in this desire and took her on.

Every Saturday she rambled out there—wearing waders to get to the place. She would unpack her rucksack and set up to draw at the observation window. After muddled attempts, she would remove herself to the rickety deck simply to watch them, standing on one leg, unconsciously curving the other behind her.

The professor corrected her drawings not as her art teacher did, but from the ready observations of the scientist who knew more about these radiant water birds than anyone. "Never apologize for an honest mistake," he would say when she muttered, "Sorry."

R revered her weathered and recondite role model—who was quite a cryptic raconteur if she caught him in the right mood. Sometimes he'd gesture to the optical illusion and say, "That's my reminder."

"Reminder of what?" she'd ask, regarding the old woman/young woman on the wall, now so familiar her eye untangled it, just as she'd begun to untangle the lines in her drawings of the egrets. Yet the illusion was still mysterious. "Reminder of what?" she'd prompt him.

Then he would sum up: "Life's reversals." And, quietly singing *Non, Je ne regrette rien*, he would announce that soon he would kick her out because it was time for his weekly stiff Rob Roy, which he intended to savor in lonesome splendor as the sun set over the swamp. Then he would say, "How I relish my solo rut!" And R would be dismissed.

Over the two years of drawing and watching the great egrets, R grew taller but no less gawky. She cut her hair in a feathery cap, got better at sketching—though nothing about drawing the great egrets was straightforward; at first they were animals, but then they became lines raveling and shadows reaching and ragged radials raking the water as they lifted their heavy bodies into the sky—better at watching, and no better at all at reconciling the professor's contradictory remarks.

"What does 'Je ne regrette rien' actually mean?" she asked one day as she finished a vivid version of another spiky head.

"I regret nothing," the professor said, approving of the sketch. But by young R's lights, the scientist seemed to regret everything. Quickly and stealthily, as a fishing bird might snatch its dinner from the water, she resolved never to regret.

After graduation, she moved to the city. Then she shot straight up to her goal of Never Regretting with a Bachelor of Science in Biology and Master's degree in Fine Arts. She began to earn design awards. Often she imagined the professor behind her, toasting her with his Rob Roy and a quick nod of approval, but she hardly ever went back to the island.

She was working up her courage to develop a portfolio for the Rare Bird Fellowship, which, like its name, was given only rarely. This was the year. She might not get the award, of course, but she would regret not trying. When the portfolio was nearly prepared, she visited the RBF Headquarters. No one at the front desk, she ventured into the nest of offices behind. There she found a formidable woman leaning over a drawing table, standing on one high heel, the other dangling off the foot curled behind her.

When the woman turned around, she peered regally over her chic glasses, regarding R's painter's pants and thick-soled sandals. "May I help you?" she said, passing a manicured hand through her dramatic white hair. Her silk suit disguised her figure in a most sophisticated way, emphasizing her long legs in black tights. She carried her age beautifully.

R, who couldn't summon words to respond, presented the half-completed portfolio. The woman pursed her very red lips.

"Yes, I see some talent," she said. "Come next week with more, R."

"How did you know my name?" R marveled.

The woman sneered. "From your huge, adolescent signature on these egrets."

R scampered out of the office and went all out on the portfolio. When she brought it back the following week, she encountered a receptionist at the front desk.

"I'd like to see—" R suddenly realized she didn't know the woman's name. After she began to describe her, the receptionist said in awe, "You must mean Madame." After a considerable wait and several tentative-sounding calls, R was led back to her.

Madame imperiously perused the drawings. "With whom have you studied?" she demanded. R rattled off the names of her teachers; hoping to bolster her credibility, she even ventured to name the professor. A distinguished scientist might help.

"Monsieur le professeur," Madame purred, "so, he is still at the Centre de la Nature?"

"Well, I think he is," R said.

"Keep going," was all Madame said. R did. She brought in her third attempt just before the deadline.

"This is getting a bit boring, don't you think? Why you are pestering me?" Madame lowered her glasses and smoothed her startlingly white hair.

"I didn't mean to pester you," R ventured, "but the Rare Bird Fellowship deadline is this week."

"Do you not think I'm aware of that?" Madame snapped as she opened the beautifully organized, complete portfolio. "You do not really mean to apply for this award, do you?"

R's silence conveyed that, of course, she did.

Madame slapped the portfolio closed. "Surely you're not serious about this application. You are too young; your work is too undeveloped. It is simple." She continued with exquisite rancor. "It is not rich. Not sophisticated. It affects old-fashioned principles. You will only be rejected. Don't do it, *ma petite* R. You will regret it."

At that R was dismissed. Undeveloped? Not serious. Too young? Too simple? Not rich enough? Unsophisticated? Redundantly out of date?

R went home and regarded her images. Revolting, all of them. Risible. Rotten. Rejectable. *Non, Je ne regrette rien!* she tried to roar alone in her room, but couldn't. Her lovely long neck hung in defeat. She regretted every heron, ibis, kingfisher, crane, stork, pelican, spoonbill, and egret she had drawn since she was a child. Of course she did not apply for the RBF.

Then came the echoes of self-recrimination. She would not have a fellowship because she hadn't even given herself a chance to be turned down. She'd run away like a rabbit. R had a fleeting mental picture of her island school classroom where the rabbit reversed to a duck. *I've . . .* she thought, *ducked my goals. Just gone off my roll toward the top and curved out and reeled back down to where I started.* She resolved never to pick up her pencils again.

The resolution didn't last. Even if she was a bad bird artist, it was the only thing she wanted to be.

R wrapped her sketchbook in plastic and fled the tall buildings for the sea-level island, putting on her waders to go out to the field station. The swamp resounded with the racket of rills and rough calls.

She found the station unlocked, but empty. Still on the

wall flapped the familiar reversible image of the old woman and the girl.

Below the observation window, among the reeds, stood a great white egret. She could not step outside and risk disturbing it, so she flipped her sketchbook open and drew, her hand taking a line for a walk around the profile of the bird.

The professor silently appeared in the doorway. "Having regrets about the city?" he asked, his voice as whiskery and rough as his face. There was something blurred about him, something undefined.

She began to weep.

"Regret doesn't mean you'd change what you've done," he said. "It's a place. The negative space a choice leaves."

Her sobs quieted as she took this in.

"Yes," he said, "you see what you did *and* what you didn't do. Both of them before your eyes. A reversible image." His hand hovered about six inches above her head almost seeming about to pat the feathered cap of her hair, then withdrew.

R blew her nose and looked down at her sketch. When she had let her hand walk around the bird's profile, she had also made an outline of her own profile, reversing it to the avian silhouette.

"My 'Great R-Egret,'" she said.

Below, the real great egret dipped and flew toward the roiling ocean.

The Sister Sailors

S sailed on her ship from the land of sparrows. *S* sailed on *her* ship from the land of swallows. S, a spouse and mother, sadly parted from her husband and child for this deployment. *S*, a solitary woman, left her distant siblings with sweet abandon. They were both about to serve overseas. Their ships sailed toward the shores of war, where their countries combined their forces, depositing troops on the same beaches.

Though the two women could not have been more different (S was homesick, *S* unbound), both were scared. The smoke of danger slithered beneath their respective cubicle doors. Neither was new to combat. Sheer experience stirred their fear. The struggle for each was to control an alarm inside, a wakened panic that took the shape of insomnia.

As it happened both came up with the same solution. They angled for nighttime guard duty on shore, where small boats secretly brought rebels to hide in the caves among the shoreline boulders. Thus it was at low tide in the pitch dark and cold that they met for the first time.

In tandem they were to patrol, armed, in buggies with searchlights. But, where the buggies couldn't roll, S and *S* had to go on foot in the night. S was stocky; *S* was slight but strong. Both about the same height, the two found it easy to assist each other as they slid, in full gear, on the seaweed and lichen-covered rocks.

It was lost on neither of them that the word *ship* sails beside the word *friend*. Just having someone at your elbow is a basis for such friendship, especially as fear sluices with every wave's slash at the shore. They feared for their limbs and their brains, for their necks and their lungs and their every organ—and staved it all off because they were seasoned, and because they weren't alone.

At watch breaks, when they crept into a beach hollow to pour coffee into their battered cups, S and *S* kidded and told each other stories. *S* teased that swallows were superior to sparrows, and S claimed the opposite. S described the stay-at-home dad and the sterling child, *S* the snake-in-the-grass siblings.

Night after night, with an elbow, a glove, with covering fire, or a suddenly gunned motor, with a strong arm for an unpredictable insurgent dug in the sand, they saved each other's lives. They were supposed to rest onboard in the daytime, and their sheer exhaustion did plunge them asleep, but they were always woken up, if not by the sailors on other schedules, then by the dreams neither volunteered to describe.

One night S stumbled, then *S* reaching for her, tripped. They slipped toward the waves, neither being able to help the other. It was only experience and the padding of the gear that stopped them on the last ledge where, half concussed, *S* called for S, and S heard *S*, and they hauled each other back over the rocks. At last up on the sand, soaked, they checked each other for injuries. S seemed to have a broken rib, and *S*'s jaw was bloodied and bruised. They were lucky.

In a state of fatigue that neither would ever be able to explain to another living being, all they wanted to do was sleep. Yet they could not. They'd lost their waterproofed communicators, they had one gun, and they'd have to keep each other awake until someone woke to their absence and came out to pick them up.

As they huddled shivering and waiting that night, the flick of a common fact between them solidified their bond even more than their injuries. It was smaller than a tiny pearl of Krazy Glue.

"What silly thing do you miss most?" *S* asked S. "Not a person, a thing."

And S replied immediately, "The dishwasher."

"The dishwasher," *S* murmured.

"Yes, after everyone's asleep," S said. "I turn it on the last thing before I go to bed."

"I turn it on last thing, too."

Their favorite sound was a swoosh, a slap-lap of foamy water, not surging into the shore, but quite contained, an ocean in a metal and plastic box. Of course their bedtimes were entirely dissimilar; one tucked herself in with a book, the other tucked in a child, then slept beside a man. But both turned the lights out, and beneath the covers on a peacetime mattress at midnight with the curtains closed against the lights of their cities, both heard the same sound. Instead of mollusks jostling in the undertow of a depth bomb, plates rattled in the swoosh of their dishwashers, S-curves of waves from the whirling sprinklers inside a kitchen appliance, the tide heated from the dials.

Slung into the sand, they found this sameness—their saving of one another shared inside a homesound's singing.

T's Diary

Truth is the job of a tree, especially one of a noble taxonomy like T, descended from the Family: Aceraceae, Species: *A. saccharum*. Like all in her genus, she became a diarist: reporting what happened every year in a ring inside her trunk. Ever since she was a little seed, twirling on an updraft, a maple key traveling through the tangled latticework of branches, the arms of her grandfather and grandmother trees, she commanded herself to tell the daily truth.

And she has done just that for two centuries. At ninety-five feet tall and a mother tree, T has tremendously deep roots—two-thirds of her is underground! And a good thing, too, given the heat. A fungus ravaged her branches one terrible year, but after a great storm came and pruned them off, she became magnificently lopsided, and her rings tell the tale of it all.

As a sapling T recorded the teaching growth (learn to surround an obstacle), and then as a slender sugar maple with a brilliant red head she told the truth of survivor grace (always bow in a storm). But there were tons of trees back then, soaking up carbon dioxide, exhaling oxygen, nourishing legions of tanagers and trilliums and generations of those who walked among her family. Then came the ones who canoed in and cut her great-great-great-grandparents to build forts, and later the drivers of horses who chopped down her friends—calling it "clearing." But when the drivers of vehicles came, they visited terror upon hundreds of thousands of her family in a centuries-long holocaust of trees, all just to wipe their derrieres.

It was a miracle T had survived the threat of the ax and the turbulence of the blizzards and the toxicity of the rainfall, not to mention the terrible year a noose hung over her outstretched branch . . . If it wasn't the ice storms, it was the hurricanes, and now the heat and drought. T wasn't a journalist, or a historian, or a meteorologist—she just recorded what happened in her diary. It was a self-portrait, really. Locked inside her central core. They'd have to chop her down to get at it.

But luckily they wouldn't do that unless absolutely necessary, for the long-gone forest has become a park. Now the foot traffic of the teeming metropolis sweeps past her, for she watches over a diagonal path that many walkers discover as a short cut. They are not aware of what she does for them. As they leave the cement and see her, they spiral down into themselves just the way a maple seed twirls down to the ground to root. She sends oxygen their way, just as she sends carbon to those younger trees. T settles a calm around them—ataraxia, the sense of well-being named by the ancients, and pretty much guaranteed to be felt by anyone who even looks at a tree.

Late one warm night a couple trysted against her trunk. They used her without thinking—a prop, inanimate they thought. When she felt against her bark the weight of their bodies, she leaned back into them as they leaned into her, an upright bark mattress. After they left, T recorded it.

When a cat fled through the park, stopping to scratch her nails on T—*ouch!*—the cat knew she was alive.

A living witness, T noted down the rainfall, the humidity, even the touch of a man who stopped to examine the initial he'd once carved into her with a penknife. *I hadn't realized my mark would scar her for so long,* he thought apologetically, amazed at how deep it seemed, now that her bark had grown up around the wound.

Should I be tracing the truth of all existence? T teased herself. But what the truth of all existence was, she didn't know. She was an old lady maple, keeping a diary like a great-grandma who totaled up her sick headaches and wash days. *To testify to the truth,* she thought, *you have to know what it is . . .* And what did she know except what had happened to her? Who in this world has the talent to paint a more trustworthy self-portrait than a tree?

A balloon and a plastic bag floated past her on a windy spring day, careful not to get snagged in her branches.

"We've got to notice trees more," said a passerby.

"And be grateful," his companion added primly.

Late one autumn afternoon, A and THE pushed little AN down the path in the stroller, passing the great T. "A maple," A said. "*The* maple," THE said, "most transcendent in the city."

Glad for that compliment, T thought, proud that she inspired awe. But she noticed that little AN was silent. The child had yet to utter a word. T felt the parents' anxiety reach over her treetop.

It was time for T to give her annual survivor party. Just after she showered down all her leaves, she sent a thought-aroma invitation for a late October gathering. Little g arrived first and tussled about in T's shed tresses, for now he collected leaves. C brought his grandson and I brought *his* grandson and they all joined g in his gleeful play with Jiggle on her way to the gym with J. From a crook of T's limbs, Maugie regarded them, having made an accommodation with several squirrels. Safe in T's highest branches, pigeons crooned.

A and THE brought AN in the stroller, their worried expressions gradually softening. T's ataraxia, that fortunate contentment beneath the shoulders of a great tree, settled around them all, swirling up in rustlegusts. The kids kicked the leaves at T's base, the adults watched the kids. They all forgot to concentrate, . . . all except wee AN, who stared with terrific intensity up into the tessellations of her branches.

"An amazing tree!" piped the little article from the stroller.

"The very first words from our little seed!" THE exclaimed.

T towered tenderly over her party, relishing her visitors and their antics as those who've witnessed tragedies can. Time transmogrified back from infinity, trellising into her trunk. *Carrying on is character*, she thought. *I'm no tragedienne.* That night, she wrote it all inside herself.

Useful U

 U loved being useful. He was a guy who could clean an eavestrough of a Saturday morning and plough through handyman chores faster than a vacuum cleaner. He was neat, too. Always swept up the sawdust from the drill, wiped up the gunk from the old plumbing he coaxed into another year, and kept his beautiful wooden worktable oiled. The table was the *pièce de résistance* of his workshop off the garage, a utopia of neatly racked hardware and tools. It stood in the center, huge and ready as a canvas for the next project.

Down a short paving-stone path from the garage was U's house—also his place of business. He was a massage therapist. The former living room had become his clinic room, where stood another beautiful table, padded and of his own design. His clients (twisted from accidents or simply the accident of pulling out a bottom desk drawer the wrong way) heaved their bodies up on this table to be fixed.

U loved his work. He was a muscular guy, but flexible. He could lift a torso from the table and turn it this way and that, returning it to the shape it was born with—until the person got injured again. Then he would lay his hands with mercy on those bones and muscles, those shoulders, that back.

One morning he woke up in the undertow of a dream. A landscape had swelled with humanoid figures seen from a tiny vantage point below, looking up toward their undulating hillock backs. The dream made him uneasy— it was all so unreal.

He rose, showered, called his lively ninety-two-year old mother, who still managed to live alone, chatted with her about her aches and pains and when he would be coming next, then met his first client—and the one after that, and after that. In his break U walked out into the bright air free of the smell of massage oil and slipped into his workshop with its smells of varnish and WD-40. Around the walls were piled neatly categorized heaps of waste materials— scrap metals, fixtures, leftover lumber, cords, and odds and ends from broken alarm clocks to toaster racks that U couldn't bring himself to throw out. *You never know*, he always thought, *they might prove useful*. The pieces stuck up at odd angles. Though U attempted to keep the twisted piles orderly, they formed an ungainly frame around the centerpiece of that oiled worktable.

As he stood there, mesmerized by the shapes in the sunlight, he wondered where had he had seen those figures in the dream before. They seemed uprooted from a place

he'd been. Time to return to his clients. But throughout
the day in the breaks between treatments, he was drawn to
thoughts of his workshop, and just before he went to bed,
he slipped out there again. The room lay in darkness, but
for the streetlight beam that illumined silhouettes.
Protruding from the heaps of stretched, wronged, and
wounded metal and lumber, sensuous shapes seemed to
reach and surge like arms.

An umbilicus to his upbringing tugged.

When he was a boy, he had been required to massage his
mother's spine with old-world unguents. He had sat on the
floor, while mother sat on a footstool. U would make long,
long strokes with his tiny hands, up and down the monument
of her spine, as if he were sanding a sculpture. He never felt
more useful and grown-up than when he helped her.

On each of these occasions she told him the source of her
ailment. She'd grown up in a war where everything ugly,
unnatural, and untoward had happened to her. It had
pushed into her, stretching her spine like a wire, and she
was never able to spring back.

Whenever U heard this story, he felt the world falling
down on him and an unbearable responsibility to heave it
back up. He heard the story often, for twice a week he
treated his mother's back.

❦

After work the next day he went to visit his tiny mother. He brought a new unguent and tried out its greaseless healing properties. "What would I do without you?" she asked, and told him again a part of her story. "I was humbled," she said, "humiliated. And I have never ever forgotten." As always, she sweetly thanked her son, and she said what she always said—"But now I have U"—and he left her cozy in her bathrobe.

The next day U felt something underlying push up through him, an urge. Perhaps it was just the energy he always felt when he had an unexpected hour after a cancelation. Back he strode to the workshop to regard the hillocks of wood and metal. Was it time to undertake a rescue of this detritus? Perhaps he could make himself useful. By now his dream, seemingly forgotten, had receded into an under-universe of *un*-forgetting. U seized one piece of wood and sanded it into . . . a *U*. He wedged a piece of wrought iron into one of his vises and began to bend it into . . . a *U*.

Then he returned to his house where the washing machine and dryer were always on, and the sheets and towels for the massage table were always warm and needing folding. He cleaned out the dryer trap and greeted his next client. But after the oils and flesh, he returned to the sanding in the workshop.

It certainly wasn't very tidy. Sawdust twirled in motes. U sneezed. *What am I doing?* he asked himself. But something he couldn't question seemed to have given him an ultimatum. He made *U* after *U*, smoothing the angled, angling the curvilinear, cementing the materials. There on the worktable a sculpture was shaping up. With its little alarm-clock head and the spiraling *U*s of its *U* shape, it looked like a boy, reaching his hands up high.

He began to spend his days going back and forth from massage table to worktable, from kneading umpteen muscles in continual misuse by ungainly people to making the unutilized into the unlikely. His dream of the figures moved sinuously through him and out his arms and hands like waves. With an urgency he never expected to feel, he also began to sculpt the other figures in the dreamscape.

Yet this didn't unsettle him. Instead, he settled in, something uncontrollable now, in his hands, controlled. Something abashed and humiliated in her, something undercut, now the underside of what he made.

But it wasn't only for her. What he began to accomplish was unique to U. Nor was it a complete U-turn from the life he had always lived. He had just incorporated the unknown into the useful.

On those late afternoons and evenings when his mother repeated her unfortunate story, one he could almost recite in unison with her, he undertook the opposite direction. What for her was uncontrolled, U controlled. Replacing the old feeling of the world falling down on him and the unbearable responsibility to heave it back up was an uncommon world, unmoored and monumental. *U*-bodies stood with an uplift, torsos undaunted.

The Plunge of V

"I'm coming with you!" V cried to Adam and Eve, "I'm taking your plunge!"

And V leapt from the place she'd been born (in the crook of a branch of the Tree of Knowledge) onto the stunned couple. She planted her imprint in the animal skins they hugged around them, creating the first primitive couture, furry V-necked vestments they could fit over their heads. Then they left the verdure of the Garden to venture into the cold.

V had to go with them. How could she stay living in innocence? She was born to be fashionable.

Through the centuries her point became more precise (especially after the invention of scissors), yet V was not interested in making points, but in *being* them.

V always pointed down toward the vestibule of the vagina, but V's pride was more than the vajayjay, it was the plunge, the valiant leap into the void.

She sprang to the wings on the helmets of the Visigoths, dove off ledges to the halls of Valhalla, folded

herself into the inner elbows of the multiple arms
of Vishnu.

V invested herself everywhere, from the *V* of the geese
in fall to the *In vino veritas* signs above the wine bar.

Revelation was V's position, even when she climbed
inside the quavers of the voices of high school valedictorians.
"I'm coming with you!" she always shouted, varooming
into their visions.

She never wanted to be left behind. She always wanted to
go forward, an arrow of a vibrant universal form—even on
something as tame as the collar of a man without a tie or the
blouse open to a woman's cleavage by just one more button.
Maintaining the adventure of flesh, she was voluptuous,
but also a little vestal. She peeked from the necklines of
Vermeer's virgins and out from the crook of the seamstress's
thumb and index finger in paintings by Vuillard.

V had the memory of the long view. She never forgot
how she vexed a vengeful deity as she leapt from innocence to
become a veritable spiritual *couturière*. Her adventure is still a
vestige of every journey. Even now V vaults onto travelers'
clothes as they revolve in suitcases turning in every baggage
carousel from Venice to Vladivostok. V burrows into each
traveler's thought of liberty and frames the chest, the breast,
the heart (even as it might reveal a scar), inserting her
valor into their vast unknown.

Wacktastic!

Why be? To witness another's existence, of course.

Wisteria was the ordinary daughter of a warlock, and Wittle was the normal son of a witch. They lived in neighboring skyscrapers across a wide West Side street. Luckily, their two windows were directly across from each other. Below, the street was busy with people and vehicles and dogs and deliveries, and all that goes on in city life.

Once wee Wittle realized there was another small being across the way, he waved, and with no hesitation little Wisteria waved right back. They made signs to one another through their high-up, firmly closed windows, and their gestures became a whole way of talking without words. Sometimes, though, they wrote big letters on the overheated steam of their windows in winter. But when the radiators clanked, the letters dripped away. In summer, when they opened the windows and tried to shout, their words wizzled off on the breeze. It turned out that signaling worked best.

The buildings they lived in were the old-fashioned kind with cast iron window frames with huge locks and comfortably wide ledges. Wisteria's building had higher maintenance fees and a much more regular window washer, a whiskery, warty fellow. Wisteria would watch him rappel along her building with his ropes and bucket, sitting on his flat board. When he got to her window, she leaned out and had a chat. Then he sailed on down, down to the street, the world.

Wittle and Wisteria were classmates in the weird school of life that was framed by two windows of two children locked in their rooms by a mother witch and a daddy warlock. As Wittle sharpened his wits on reading, Wisteria wrote. And the warty window washer whizzed by.

One day Wittle saw that across the street the warlock was wrenching Wisteria's elbow. He saw her wince. He saw her wilt.

Later that day he saw the cast on her arm.

That night he saw the warped warlock in remorse bring Wisteria a West Highland terrier puppy.

From *her* window Wisteria would often see the witch racking up yet another spell on Wittle, sure she could wrangle the normal boy into witchcraft. Wisteria saw Wittle drink each brew. She air-spelled *WOOZY?* She watched as he waggled, wobbled, and wove back and forth in the throes of the whopping potions. She signaled *WHOA!*

Years winnowed the two of them. Years whammed them. Years wrung Wittle and Wisteria up into a young man and a young woman. The West Highland terrier learned his tricks at a whistle. Wisteria could have become a waif, or worse, a wraith, but instead she became willowy and a little bit wild. Years of woe became years of woo.

They could have whined, and some times they did. But they wallowed in their *Weltschmerz* together. Well, as together as two individuals signaling from window to window can be. Watched by a dog. And a warty, whiskery window washer.

Wittle could have become a wimp, but instead he became a wrestler of thoughts, and, recently, a wrencher of wire. One of the witch's failed attempts to whorl him into a wizard had yielded a long, thick many-plied wire. He hooked it up in his room and entertained himself by walking across it. Day after day he raised the wire, first from the heat registers, then to the doorknobs, and last to the plant hooks in the ceiling.

Wisteria signaled *WISH*.

Wittle signaled *WANT*. He hurled the wire across the street, and missed.

Wisteria shrugged *WHOOPS*.

Wittle waved *WAIT*. He hurled it again. And again.

The window washer watched. He waved to Wisteria. And began to position his board and ropes.

Wisteria gesticulated *WHEN?*

Wittle frowned *WORRIED.*

Wisteria motioned *WASHER.*

Wittle hurled the wire again, and this time the whiskery, warty fellow caught it and helped Wisteria secure it to the iron window lock. Wittle crept out over the traffic. By the time he thought, *Don't wuck everything up,* he had whizzed across the wire!

The Westie jumped into the basket where Wisteria had packed her notebooks, and the window washer began to lower them all to the street.

"My worthy," Wisteria whispered.

"My wonder," Wittle whispered.

Once they got down, they donned the disguises the window washer had brought them: the big white aprons they'd wear at Waffle World where jobs awaited them. They'd have to learn to live by their wits. But, really, they had already been doing that. For them it was quite normal to outwit a witch and a warlock. But it wasn't quite normal to say "love." They wouldn't say *that* for a long, long time, not till they left their jobs at Waffle World after Wisteria sold the film rights to her memoir.

But right now, balancing on the window washer's board, shocked at the sound of each other's voices, they became immediately shy and reverted to gestures until they reached the street.

Wisteria mouthed *WHEEEE!*

And Wittle pointed from himself to her, *WE*.

"Now watch that bucket!" warned the window washer.

Woof barked the Westie.

X Marks Her Spot (with Lipstick)

When X got home from her brush with mortality—just a little quadruple bypass—she decided that her new heroines would be exceedingly vigorous and mature despite pesky ailments like heart trouble. She chose two. One came from the afterlife: Diana Vreeland (who mounted a dozen costume exhibits *extraordinaires* before her heart failed at eighty-six). Among the still living, she took as a heroine the spirited Diana Athill, celebrated editor and memoirist, keeping up her elucidating correspondence at ninety-six. These exquisite women were not exempt from death, obviously, but they made the ends of their lives into excursions, in mind if not in body—artistic, fashionable, spiritual brief adventures.

Because both Diana A. and Diana V. advised the wearing of makeup in advanced age, X decided to make a short excursion of her own to an exclusive makeup counter, one of those exorbitant places that, to her, was both exhilarating and exhausting. She was determined to try to exhume a

shade of lipstick she'd worn many years ago. Colors always come back from exile.

Now X didn't want to exaggerate the momentousness of this adventure, but at the makeup counter she thought she might find the perfect spot between life and death, the place of *x*-ing out, the border crossing, so to speak.

A sparkling young man helped her explore all the different shades, but she could not find her old fave, Extravaganza, a honey hue. The best he could do was Xanadu. Just a particle different. Slightly more evolved. As anything reincarnated into the next level of life would be.

The end of existence, it's just external, isn't it? That's what X now thought. When you expire, she believed, you just transform. You extricate yourself from human form and start to become something else. A nice cloud of ashes to scatter downwind, she hoped, and not in the face of whoever threw them. Or a nice bit of compost.

Long ago X began to explore the great traditions, the ones that attempt to explain life and death. As advised by her teachers, she started with Socrates. After she examined what Epicurus and Epictetus had to say (that took her college years), she expended her young woman's energy on the exasperating truths of Buddha. It was only as she aged that they began to make excellent sense to her. Of course, she found ideas about the here and the hereafter in the Bible. And more in the Bhagavad Gita. But so many of the ideas overlapped. Where did they come from, anyway?

How did they circulate? They weren't *ex nihilo*. This persuaded her toward reincarnation.

There was a way, she slyly thought, that major ideas were just like minor lipstick colors. They kept circulating, going into exile, so to speak, each one an exemplar of a color for a season, and then slightly altered for the next season, and you just waited for them to come back, as if returning from a trip abroad. Ideas were never truly extinct. Take passive resistance, for example. Or even the rotten ones, like misogyny. They *seemed* to be extinguished, but then they came back! Some thoughts she wished would just exit permanently. (And some colors be extirpated, too.) Yet you couldn't exorcise them. Even an execrable idea comes back and seems exotic to those who've never experimented with it. Ideas were like stars blinking on and off. Or moon phases.

The night sky excited X—and appalled her. The immensity. The vastness of it. She was so small. Smaller than a sequin. Than a dot. A minim. She was like a molecule. A nanosecond. How could an *X* mark her spot? What was she worth? Her insignificance used to terrify her. Yet here at the makeup counter, among the many mirrors and the choices of colors whose caps sparkled like the stars, reflecting and refracting, *she was.* X knew her spot. Right in that mirror. Even though she was a fleck, she was a world.

Perhaps, she reasoned, passing *out* of the mirrored world was like passing *into* the universe—being exported out there among all the other ideas.

She liked the fact that she was having notions that others had had centuries before, that they somehow were being passed on to her, as if through the air. Inspired by the exhalations of breath from centuries past, she felt strangely secure in a translucent chain of being, each link pale but evident, like shades of moonlight. *Which do I prefer, the sun or the moon?* X asked herself. *Which one, the thing clearly seen—or the thing in mystery?*

"Would you like the Xanadu to replace the Extravaganza?" asked the sparkling young man at the counter.

"I'll try Xanadu," she replied. "Let's experiment." With a mental wave to the living Diana A., she continued on her expedition, crossing the universe (eventually) toward her other heroine, Diana V., and well beyond.

yet, Yes

When *y*s are young, their leg hangs below the line, and curves, and they slalom around on it happily until the curve gradually straightens, and then, in a Herculean coming-of-age effort, they make a capital leap to live the rest of their lives on top of the line.

But somehow y's leg had never straightened; it had never lost its curve. Even though he was quite grown up, he lived half below the line. He often felt guilty, and couldn't always enjoy all that was yelicious and yonderful.

"I put my foot in everything—yech!" y said to his partner Y, a regular Capital, at breakfast.

Y was placing yolk-perfect eggs before y with his slender hands, black hairs curling enticingly over the knuckles. "Not in everything. You put your foot through *one thing*, and you've magnified it a yillion times."

y hopped over to the cupboard to get the jelly, ruffling the darling heads of their two adopted girls with yogurt mushed about their faces. Then he returned to his place, setting before him a group of photographs he had gotten up to look at again in the middle of the night.

"Put those damn photographs away!" his incredulous partner insisted, "Tear them up. AND delete them. Whenever you can't sleep, you get them out and you decide you're solely responsible!"

"Yes, I am," y sighed, "because if it's somebody's fault then there's a reason for being."

"*What!*" Y fumed. "Two reasons for being are playing with their yogurt right this minute! Not to mention yours truly."

"You're right," y said, "Yet. I can never rectify it all . . . I left. I just left him there." It was always *Yet* with y.

His father had simply ignored the fact that his son's leg never straightened. "Belly up to the line!" he would say to y. And one day Y Senior said even worse, "Climb up onto the roof!"

Father had fixed that roof when Grandfather was too old to climb, and now, when Father was too old, young y was supposed to. But when y tried to balance, his foot slipped through the wood rot up to his groin. His nails and hammer flew. It took sheer adrenalin and many attempts to lift his torso up through the shingles and crawl to a safe beam to look down at Father, yowling out his disappointment, and worse, disgust, but certainly no concern.

And that was when y left home.

He climbed carefully down from the roof and, lucky he still had a leg to stand on, traveled to this faraway city where he found his new home and his job. He embraced his good fortune at sharing it all with a man with beautiful arms, and with little Yuki and Yukon, now both with yogurt in their hair and yodeling in the way that little *y*s yell, and with their Yorkie yapping, and the domestic yawp continuing.

"Every day isn't as yawful as you'd have it be, you know," Y said. (They were yin and yang in the glass-half-full or half-empty department.)

That roof never was fixed. Yahoos got in. With their yucky paw prints still on the walls and beds, y's father, in an act of pure frustration at his son who failed to honor the Laws of Yesteryear and just use his willpower to get up on the damn line, tore it down. And in an unfortunate fluke of timing, y's old high school friend had driven out yonder, past the house, seen the demolition, and e-mailed him the photos.

A year passed. y's father refused his frantic calls.

More years. y took up yoga. His father refused his infrequent calls.

Eventually Y Senior died of Inability to Yield. y delivered the eulogy.

Now it was another yuletide. y wiped his daughters' little chins and listened to their yakety-yak while Y watched him eat his yummy meal.

"You made your stand," Y said. Y had said this to his beloved y twenty-five times. He said it buttercup soft and dandelion brash. He brayed it as if a tawny hound. But y never seemed to hear him fully.

Yet on this morning y absorbed the statement. Having run through nearly an alphabet of excuses, he heard at last what fit him to the letter and understood the why of what he'd done.

"When my leg crashed through the roof, I thought I ran away from the damage, but, really, I stood up against it all."

"Yes! So throw those pictures out," his partner said.

A leg is a base, whether it's on the line or below the line, or no longer exists except in the mind, y thought flexibly, before he deleted the photos, breaking the final yoke. Later, as their two little yodelers practiced their carols, y mixed the Yorkshire pudding, and Y gave him a little shoulder massage. *Mmmmm, yes.*

Z at the Satisfactory

Like a very slow zipper closing link by link,
the box turtle left a track through the glade,
passing old Z's bungalow, heading toward the
road. The long retired zoologist observed the
tetrapod. *Just my speed*, Z thought. Z was still on call at
the Herpetological Rescue Center and made his bungalow
a stopgap resting place for abandoned or injured creatures.
Until yesterday he'd harbored a Zanzibar gecko with a
bright blue tail. But the gecko's new host (Z never liked
the term *owner*) had picked up the reptile, and now his
bungalow was empty. *Good*, Z thought, *I need a rest.* He
watched as the *Terrapene carolina bauri* headed straight
onto the macadam.

But what about the cars? Z panicked. Out he hobbled
into the road to stop traffic, but the animal seemed
oblivious. It went on, not fretting that its life lay in the
path of violence—it had its own bizness to do. Z waved
his arms at the cars, "Ztop! Ztop!" and the traffic
halted while the turtle safely crossed. Then Z stood

at the side of the road watching the turtle make its way into the glade.

Ever the observer, Z just couldn't resist following it.

The dome-backed reptile led him deeper and deeper into the moist green light. A zephyr zithered its musical breeze. He tracked the critter, slowly, zlowly . . . Z was past his zipping and zooming days.

After a long, long time a leafy ziggurat appeared.

So it does *exist!* thought the old man.

There it was: the Satisfactory, the sweetest manufacturing plant of all.

So, it's not a myth . . . Z had heard rumors about the Satisfactory all the time from the botanists at the lab, but plants hadn't been his field.

The turtle slowly nodded its head before it went its horizontal way, motioning toward the top of the ziggurat. Through the half-light sprouted what looked like smokestacks. Z indulged in a bit of zoolatry and took his cue from that leisurely nod. Despite his creaky joints, he seemed to find the energy to climb.

As he ascended higher and higher through the greeny haze, an exhaustion unlike any he had ever known zapped him. Z felt about a zillion years old. He heaved, zlipping and zlopping. Using his last bit of zest to crawl to the zenith, he made it.

There he rested, inspecting the tall greeny columns. They weren't smokestacks at all. They were welcoming

slides, green and inviting as reeds, hollow and cushioned. With a second wind, and ever the scientist, he couldn't resist experimenting. He slipped into one.

Down he zlid, hollering *zyzzyva-a-a-a-a!*

Zhud!

He found himself deep in the belly of the Satisfactory.

Light filtered through its living walls.

All around him lay letters, why, they were just like himself—tired and limp from living. The letters zlumped, zprawled, and zlouched in leafy loungers. The Satisfactory served for his fellow letters as his bungalow served for the critters he fostered. It was a spa of rejuvenation, a treehouse-y rest stop where those required to stand all their lives met the pleasure of being sat down and succored by fronds.

Z watched as they loosened and lightened, emancipated, beaming and calm, and he, too, began to beam in response. He thought of how much of his existence he'd spent zinging into place, just like charging into the road to ztop traffic that morning. *What if I just didn't have to zing for a time?* he asked himself. He put his observational skills to use. The *Y*s weren't yodeling, he noticed, nor were the *X*s xylating. The *W*s didn't wassail, the *V*s didn't vibrillate. Neither did the *U*s ululate, or *T*s timbrellate. Inside the Satisfactory, as Z surveyed, *S*s needn't simulate, *R*s needn't roll. He noted that the *Q*s could quell and the *P*s simply be pooped. *O*s eased their buttons.

All the letters were relaxing.

Z found a spot in an inner lounge in the midst of *N*s who had ztopped nudging and *M*s who had ztopped merging. A repast was laid on a grassy banquet table near a group of liberated *L*s and softly keening *K*s. As Jell-O slid down the throats of *J*s, *I*s ate ice cream. An *H* drank a soothing herbal tisane, while a *G* imbibed ginger tea. An *F* lay fainting next to a heavy-eyed *E*. *D*s dozed. Here a *C* quaffed a *café au lait*; there a *B* bowed over a bowl of borscht.

An *A* had fallen asleep with a piece of apple pie almost slipping from a plate. Z caught the plate and put it on a ferny end table. Then he tucked into the zabaglione and drank a glass of Zinfandel.

After his meal, Z, too, took a nap—not for a quick shuteye, but for an immeasurable ztretch of time. A bottomless rest. Z proved the heaviest snoozer of them all, emitting a steady stream of z-z-z-z-zs from his slumber. He slept what seemed a geological age, deep as the core of the earth.

Each layer of sleep returned him to the essential fact of himself. And the longer he slept, the smaller he got . . . smaller and zmaller until he was just a whit of a letter, a wizp, a fraction of his old being.

When he reached his tiniest essence, he bobbed in place for a while, breathing deeply, and then he began the long, long float up to the surface of waking. He zigged and he zagged, borne on somnolent currents that lightened and glowed until . . .

Zounds! Wee z was awake at last, renewed and ravenous. As soon as his fresh eyes adjusted, he zoomed to the breakfast bar and devoured a diminutive zucchini muffin. z's future was in the air, his next life story. What would he become? Plant? Animal? He couldn't wait to grow into himself.

Even though he was hardly more than a particle, z felt part of a plan—and the fact that the plan would never be revealed to him made him insatiably curious. He revved up his infinitesimal engine of energy, determined to find his new place in the world.

With the zest of the inquisitive, z zoomed past the sleeping letters in the belly of the Satisfactory, toward the green entrance. On the whoosh of an updraft he zipped back up the reed. Zappety-zap, he was airborne! Though he was but a speck, his eyes were sharp—look:

Through the green of the glade lay a sparkling pond.

Inside each of the multitude of drops that made up the pond swam a spangle of a reborn letter. The current carried him toward it, and z dove in—Zplash!—received by a droplet of water. He had slipped back into the alphabet.

Soon z would embody the first word of his next life. What would he pick? *Naming my first word*, he considered, *will be my most original act this lifetime.* He lay back to float and consider. Because he had all the time in the world— nothing was hurrying him—he entered a zone of pure choice. Words glided past from zeppelin to zodiac. Perhaps he could choose contemplatively with zen? Make a zany selection? Zombie? Or zedonk? *Let passion be my guide!* thought he. And at that, z's word appeared.

Zygote, the infant zoologist decided, *the first unit of life—of course!* If there was one thing he'd learned at the Satisfactory, it's that the beginning is always in the end. Zeal sealed his fate.

ACKNOWLEDGEMENTS

Alphabetique is not only a collaboration between a writer and
an illustrator, but between a writer and her editor, and an
illustrator and her art director. As a quartet, we moved forward
into the music of this book. The first notes of the tales began as
poems. Then they transformed into stories, as if from space to
time, with the radiant guidance of editor Lara Hinchberger.
When the tales became formed in their imagery, CS Richardson,
art director and author of the inspired abecedarian novel,
The End of the Alphabet, stepped in with a brilliant layout. He
then encouraged the visual poems of Kara Kosaka, collages that
not only realized the images in the tales, but magically returned
the stories to their imaginative source. It was an enchanted
intuitive process, one that held us in thrall as it took place, and
we all thank each other from the bottoms of our hearts.

Some of the very early verse versions were published in the following literary journals: *Barrow Street, Cerise, Margie, Painted Bride Quarterly, PN Review, Poemlemon, Poetry International, Rattle, River Styx, The Southampton Review,* and *Washington Square.* The current versions of "The Poet" and "Q's Quest" appeared in *Poetry.* Thank you Kathleen Anderson for representing this book. Thank you Anne Holloway for your copyeditor's conjuring. Thank you Ruta Liormonas for your steady hand as *Alphabetique* enters the world. Thanks always to Mike Groden and to Phillis Levin.

Molly Peacock is a poet, essayist, and nonfiction writer. Her latest work of nonfiction is *The Paper Garden: Mrs. Delany Begins Her Life's Work at 72.* She is also the author of the memoir *Paradise, Piece by Piece.* Her most recent collection of poems is *The Second Blush.* She serves as the Series Editor of *The Best Canadian Poetry in English* and as a Contributing Editor to the *Literary Review of Canada.* One of the creators of New York's Poetry in Motion program, she co-edited *Poetry In Motion: One Hundred Poems From the Subways and Buses.* She is also the editor of an anthology of essays, *The Private I,* and the author of a book about reading poetry, *How to Read a Poem and Start a Poetry Circle.* Widely anthologized, her work appears in *The Oxford Book of American Poetry, The Best of the Best American Poetry,* and *The Best American Essays.* A dual citizen of the US and Canada, Molly Peacock is a former New Yorker who makes her home in Toronto with her husband, two cats, and a jam-packed terrace garden. Visit Molly at www.mollypeacock.org.

ABOUT THE ILLUSTRATOR

Kara Kosaka is a designer and illustrator who loves the aesthetic of collage. She holds a BFA in New Media from Ryerson University, where she developed her interest in book cover design; her debut was the cover of Kate Taylor's award-winning novel, *Madame Proust and the Kosher Kitchen*. Kara's passion for art began at an early age, thanks to her mother and the love that she shared with Kara for art in its many forms – from foreign films to art galleries and fabric stores. Kara lives with her husband and daughter in the Greater Vancouver area, where she works for a local art publishing company and is pursuing her next book project. Visit Kara at www.karakosaka.com.

Alphabetique is set in Tribute, a modern typeface produced in 2003 by the German type designer Frank Heine. Heine used a single printed source – a photocopy of a reprint of a type specimen printed in the 16th century – as his model. Said specimen was set circa 1560 by the French punch-cutter François Guyot. Less influential than such masters as Garamond or Griffo, Guyot's unusual treatment of certain characters and overall idiosyncratic approach appealed to Heine's ambition: to design a font based on a Renaissance Antiqua. By referencing a poor quality third generation source (in effect a copy of a copy of a 450-year-old original), Heine had the freedom to develop a decidedly contemporary interpretation while still maintaining a link to the past.

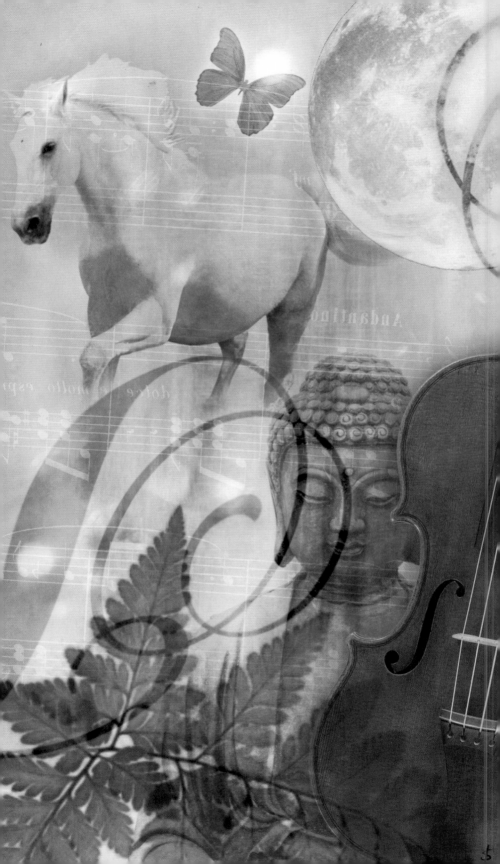